HOW TO SURVIVE A NATURAL DISASTER

HOW TO
SURVIVE
A NATURAL
DISASTER

Margaret Hawkins

THE PERMANENT PRESS
Sag Harbor, NY 11963

For information, address:
    The Permanent Press
    4170 Noyac Road
    Sag Harbor, NY 11963
    www.thepermanentpress.com

Library of Congress Cataloging-in-Publication Data

    Hawkins, Margaret—
        How to survive a natural disaster / Margaret Hawkins.
            p. cm.
        ISBN 978-1-57962-204-6 (alk. paper)
            1. Domestic fiction. I. Title.

    PS3608.A89345H69 2010
    813'.6—dc22   2010019635

Printed in the United States of America.

ACKNOWLEDGMENTS

Thanks to Ragdale, the artists' retreat that so generously provided time and space while I worked on this book, to Judith and Martin Shepard for publishing it, and to Fritz for sorting out my impossible geography.

"Light under bushel burn house down."

—MARK VONNEGUT
The Eden Express

PART ONE

MAY

I didn't speak until I was seven. I didn't feel the need. For almost half my life—I'm nineteen now—head nods and shakes were sufficient, indicating yes or no, and the occasional wail worked as an alarm when things didn't go my way. Other than that I kept my own counsel as my grandma liked to say.

We're all sitting in the yellow kitchen of our yellow house in Park View eating Sunday breakfast the first time Grandma Jack makes this observation, she and Roxanne and Craig and April on the distressed antique ladder-back chairs left over from Roxanne's first marriage, and me in April's old bird's-eye maple Amish high chair which has been set next to the granite-topped kitchen island so they can keep an eye on me. We live in a leafy suburb north of Chicago known for its granite-topped kitchen islands as well as its excellent schools, a place where smoking in public is illegal, which is why Grandma Jack never takes us out to breakfast. So here we are at the kitchen table, with omelets for them and a pile of cinnamon Cheerios for me. "That baby keeps her own counsel," Grandma Jack says again, taking a long slow drag on her Marlboro Light and meeting my gaze through a haze of smoke.

Talking didn't interest me. It was what other people did and something they did so thoroughly and constantly there was nothing for me to add. I preferred to be quiet and entertain my own thoughts and for that matter my own visitors who were invisible to everyone else and communicated in subtler ways than words. People equate speech with intelligence but when you think about it you have to admit it doesn't always work that way. Usually it doesn't, if truth be told. I had nothing I wanted to add to the general din around me.

People thought I was slow, of course—*developmentally disabled* is how I later learned they put it or, behind my mother's back, *retarded*. They watched how I stared at the plush animals in my crib and how, instead of prattling in some cute made-up language, scolding and instructing them, I stroked their polyester fur, patted and sniffed them and pressed them to my face. They watched how, when taken to the park to play with other children, I didn't, and instead lay down in the grass alone and blew on the leaves and let the bugs walk across my bare legs without crying. They thought it strange that I turned my back on the television to sit cross-legged on the floor and watch the laundry spin in a circle in the dryer as I hummed along, not with any nursery rhyme but in tune with the vibration of the machine.

They assumed I didn't speak because I didn't know how. They thought my brain didn't work—*bad early nutrition, poor little brown thing with eyes like coffee beans* I could hear them think—and that I didn't notice things even though, as I tried to tell them later, it was what I did notice that kept me silent. I could see they felt sorry for me, the teachers and baby sitters, the women in the grocery store who glanced sympathetically at Roxanne as she wheeled me up and down the aisles with my pudgy brown legs sticking straight out the front of the cart. I turned this pathos to my advantage, getting them to give me things just by staring. They gave me little juice boxes with bendable straws sticking out, crackers spread with soft cheese, Cheerios that grew damp in my palm when I closed my fist over them, cookies with holes in the center that I wore on my fingers like rings. I ate it all and grew fat and it made them happy to give me these things, it made them feel superior and warm and satisfied in their generosity. Then they patted me on the head and went back to whatever they'd been talking about.

Back then I didn't know that slow meant something bad, not right away at least. I thought slow was nice, like the way a caterpillar moved on the ground under the swing when you sat still or how April's box turtle Magellan approached the pretzel

12

I stuck into his glass tank—April said it was OK because he was an omnivore, as long as you bit the salt off first. Or how honey came out of the top of the bear, slow but sure. What's wrong with that? Only later did I realize that slow was a slight, only later did it occur to me to be offended by this confusion of silence with stupidity, this belief that just because I didn't talk I couldn't and couldn't understand what they were saying. Because let's face it, stupid is what they meant. Dumb equals dumb or so they thought.

Back then I was happy to let them do all the talking, or if not happy then resigned, at least until I reached the age of reason, when I reasoned it was time to finally speak, time to call the police and tell them what had happened.

I was born Esmeralda forty miles outside Lima, Peru, the second child of a fifteen-year-old girl named Maria and a man named Paulo who was my father and my grandfather both. I see from the forms in my file that I was a healthy baby except for an infection that caused yellow pus to form in my left eye, attracting dogs and insects and causing it to swell shut. When I was four months old my mother, who I don't remember except for the idea of a memory of the smell of cooking on her skin, rode a bus to take me to a doctor and left me there to get better. When she came back the next week to collect me he told her I was dead. By then I'd been sent to an orphanage and three months later I was on a plane to Chicago, traveling in a pink sling against my second mother's chest, my head between her large swaying breasts under a T-shirt that smelled of smoke and sweat and skin cream.

She, Mother, Mommy, Mom, Roxanne, cried for the entire plane ride home, and I must have felt her chest heave and heard her sob as she rubbed her cheek against the top of what she later described as my silky head. For my part I am told I almost didn't cry at all and maybe then was when I got the idea to keep quiet. *What was the point?* She had the crying thing covered in spades.

The flight was seven hours long. The meal was chicken cacciatore, the landing was rough. Roxanne staggered off the plane, stiff and swollen-faced from crying and dying for a cigarette. No one was there to meet us.

You may wonder how I, who was an infant when these things occurred, can know all this and all that happened next. I will tell you. Some things I remember, some things I have researched and some things I was told. I know about my first mother and the eye infection because Roxanne saved the file though in the file it says my mother never came back to collect me. I know about the flight home because Roxanne saved the pink spiral notebook she took with her to Lima, the one in which she wrote down everything that happened. I know about the T-shirt she wore and the pink sling she carried me in because she taped the Polaroid they took at the orphanage inside the notebook and put it in a big brown envelope she kept in a locked desk drawer. As for the sweat, and smoke and skin cream, she always smelled like that.

But there are other things I simply know, since knowing, or divining as you might call it, is the gift we who don't speak have been given in exchange for the friends we fail to make. So long as I didn't speak I knew things others didn't and I haven't forgotten them. That's all over now though. I let it go, gave up my birthright to silence when I called for help and now the gift is gone. But I remember. Anyway, about this story, you'll have to take my word for it.

IN MY second life here in America, in this neatly landscaped suburb, I was the second child. April was my elder and I was the silent second who soaked up all her noise. This is my second family. Roxanne is my second mother, and I am her second chance. Craig is my second father although really he is just Craig and Roxanne wouldn't want to hear me say it but I like him better for it. I am the second, and the word suggests something less than first, second best, secondhand, secondary. A dueler's second is neither daring nor principled, he's the helpful, harmless, watchful aide whose duty is to broker reconciliation without violence. Failing that, he's there to hold the guns.

April was five when they brought me home. I was a gift for her, a living doll, as far as she was concerned though one she couldn't return, and Roxanne swore to us both that I was what April had wished for on her birthday candles only a month before. There is a picture of us together taken one week after I arrived, at the welcome party they held at the church, a picture my mother kept on her bureau for years, unframed and curling at the edges and propped against a lamp. It shows April on the church steps with me in her lap, sitting under a hand-painted sign that says *Welcome Home Baby May!* April's arms are wrapped tightly around my short thick body in a hug intended either to squeeze the breath out of me or to keep me from falling. She wears a face-stretching grin that's almost a grimace and shows off her wide-spaced stubby white teeth.

Everything about April is light. Though it is late in May and the weather has been unseasonably warm, her skin is unfazed by the sun and looks like pink milk while her thin hair, which is pulled flat against her head into two pony tails that sprout sideways above either ear, has simply turned white. Even sitting down, in her yellow shorts and tank top, you can see that her body is shaped like a stick, that her joints are bumps where the branches come out. At the center of all this lightness bulges the clot of light-stopping gravity that is me. I wear some tube-like garment out of the top of which squeezes my widest part like cream from the top of a chocolate cannoli, my dark unsmiling face. It is broad, brown and flat and surrounded by a fringe of shiny black hair. I am as somber as the pope, as smooth as a bean and as brown as a berry my grandmother says, tapping her purplish fingernail against the photo three times. In contrast with April who looks transparent and appears, like some benign dragon, to breathe light out of her stretched-open mouth,

I am dense and dark—a stone, a football, a thick captured animal—and, if we both were thrown from the same window, it appears that April would float like a moth while I would sink like a sandbag. I stare straight at the camera, which is held by Grandma Jack.

"That baby studies people," she said the first time we met, fastening one squinting eye on me as she considerately pressed her creased lips shut and turned her head away to expel smoke out of the little blowhole she'd opened at the side of her mouth. "Yes you do," she said, poking me in the stomach. "You study people."

Thoughts on being the second, the younger, the youngest: it makes you watchful. It makes you calculate. It makes you compare. You have to, you're always the outsider, the Johnny-come-lately, the next in line, waiting for your number to be called. Those you admire and whose esteem you covet will always expect less of you than you are and the best you can do is to surprise them out of their low opinion of you, but that is cold comfort compared to the faith and esteem and dare I say love that you wished had been yours to begin with. To be the youngest is a lifelong lesson in unrequited love. In waiting. They, your elders, even if only by months, give you advice, condescend to you, tell you you are coddled, then write you off.

Oh not that I wasn't loved. Of course I was, I know that. Everyone told me so. They spoke of it constantly in my house and in my church, love love love, all you need is love, that big indiscriminate soup. I was loved before I ever arrived, I was often told, though particularly before I arrived it sometimes seemed to me. No one ever mentioned the unmentionable, the hierarchy of love. Or the cost. I'd been brought in, like an expert, to fix Roxanne's life.

Don't get me wrong. Roxanne meant well. Her heart, as they say, was in the right place. I'm not claiming that I don't feel a sick tug of longing sometimes, remembering how it was, the tender little songs she whispered into my soft ears, the little dresses she put me in and fluffed around my stubby legs, the way she'd kiss

16

the soles of my tiny feet and bury her tear-slicked face in the silk of my neck to inhale my skin and murmur *you are my sunshine my only sunshine.* I know she loved me. But the responsibility to love her back, love her only, became too heavy. It was my job to choose, between her and Craig, and I gave up. Love seemed too dangerous. She thinks I don't forgive her, but she's wrong, twice, she's not the one I need to forgive. I've come to understand she tried her best. It was April who was my idol and my obstacle, the one whose respect I coveted and could not win.

My mother—Craig had no say in it—changed my name to Esme though I would have preferred she kept Esmeralda and called me Jewel, which is what it means. I suppose the new name was meant to refine the old one, meant to update that greasy corn tortilla reeking Spanish with a sophisticated twist, but they ended up calling me May. May as in Maya, May as in maybe, Mother May I, may or may not, may as in might, the contingent auxiliary verb. I was May, named for the month I arrived, the month that follows April.

I looked it up. May indicates that someone has a legal or moral right to do something. Which I did, finally. But I digress.

We waited a long time to be picked up at that airport terminal, as Mother, Mommy, Mom, Roxanne became more and more agitated, punching buttons on her cell phone and whispering tremulously to me in words both gentle, when having to do with me, and obscene when having to do with Craig. Or Dad as I was told to call him and then told not to and then told to again until she finally gave up because I didn't talk anyway. Craig, Dad, Daddy, Father, Daddy Craig, that son of a fucking bitch prick father of yours. Then we went home in a cab.

APRIL

We planned to meet them, really we did, but Craig got the arrival time wrong. Then he stopped somewhere and left me in the back seat with the windows cracked while he went inside for a long time—he said it wouldn't be long but it was—and after that I started having *a bad day* as they used to say and it didn't help that we forgot to eat breakfast.

I was out of my mind I was looking forward to meeting May so much. Finally I was going to have a sister, which is what I'd always wished for, according to my mother. In fact I already had a sister they told me, a little girl who was born to be my sister except in another country and she was coming all this way home to be mine. *A sister is a friend for life.* That's what the pillow in my room said. They gave it to me when they told me about her. Later they gave me another one that said *Sisters by Chance, Friends by Choice* and then they gave me another one that said *Sisters are Blossoms in God's Garden of Love.* The people at my mother's church made them for me, embroidering the letters stitch by stitch with their stiff bumpy old hands. *All right* I said at the baby shower they held at the church two weeks before May arrived, waving my arms around in a way that made every-body laugh, *I get it. I'm happy I have a sister so bring this kid home all right already.* Everybody laughed again. They said I was the cutest, and so smart for only five.

It's true we weren't as ready for her as we should have been but we did try. In the weeks before she went to pick May up Mom was kind of shaky and she cried a lot but she got Craig to paint the room pink and the church gave us a shower and the ladies brought lots of little outfits for May and bigger, matching ones for me so I wouldn't be jealous, and Mom stopped smoking for awhile and Grandma Jack said she'd try to stop at least at our house which she ended up not being able to do but it was nice of her to offer. I made a welcome card and put some of my stuffed animals in the crib. I put in Doody and Curious George who were not my favorites but not my least favorite either and at the last minute I gave her Judy, the stuffed purple M&M, which I liked a lot.

I thought I'd love her right away and I tried but she wasn't as cute as I thought she'd be. She was just so small and quiet, staring at me all the time with her shiny black eyes. *God bless her, that baby studies people* the pastor said, the first time he saw her when he came over, with carry-out chicken chow mein and fortune cookies, to pray with us. He acted like he'd thought of it even though he'd just overheard Grandma Jack say it in the kitchen five minutes before. It was true though. She did study people. It made them uncomfortable.

My fortune cookie said *you will achieve great fame.*

CRAIG

It didn't help matters any that I didn't show up at the airport, I'll be the first to admit, especially since Jack couldn't make it. She was having some sort of *medical procedure* as she called it and wouldn't tell us what it was. So it was all on me and I blew it. I see now that I should have risen to the occasion. As Roxanne likes to put it, I was in asshole mode. To be fair though, in my own defense, I have to say I didn't mean to blow it off. I meant in fact to get things back on track, start over, bring flowers etcetera. Act the part of the proud father. I take that back. I don't mean act. I was a proud father or at least I was working on trying to become one. I wanted Roxanne to see that, to see I'd installed the infant-sized rear-facing car seat she'd told me to buy. I wanted her to see the pink stains on my jeans from painting the nursery. I'd even bought a box of cigars though Jack was the only one I knew who'd smoke them.

I'd told Karen the week before that I was breaking it off. I said I meant it this time and she agreed it was the right thing to do and reminded me she'd already broken it off two weeks before, but then when she called that morning to congratulate me on becoming a father I thought I should go see her to calm her down but I couldn't leave April at home so I took her along—I figured she was a big enough girl to stay in the car for just a few minutes and we'd go straight to the airport after that, though Karen's apartment wasn't exactly on the way. But one thing led to another and April got upset being left alone—it really wasn't for that long—so then we had to stop at McDonald's to get French fries and hot chocolate to calm her down and by the time we got to the airport they were gone. I guess I had my cell phone turned off, by mistake I swear, and I think I may have gotten the arrival time wrong. Roxanne was pretty upset and I don't blame her.

I know everyone thinks I'm an asshole. And I guess they're right, though I don't see it. I think of myself as a nice guy, maybe too nice a guy, always going an extra mile to please some girl.

In my own defense I have to say that I feel like I was drafted. I never meant things to go this far and I think I deserve some credit for staying as long as I did. In fact I always thought I was pretty loyal, considering. Considering how much I didn't want to be there. You've got to take that into account, how far someone is coming from to appreciate how much effort they've put into getting there. What I mean is I could have split and run a hundred times. I wanted to split and run a hundred times—a thousand times—but I didn't. I stayed. I think I deserve some credit for that.

She knew I had misgivings from the start. Wait and see, she kept saying. Give it time. If it's God's plan it will all work out. One thing I've learned—when Roxanne starts talking about God's plan she usually means her own.

What can I say? I was just a kid. Well, maybe not a kid, I was twenty-nine. But I was a young twenty-nine, and I was lost. Roxanne took over my life and at first I was flattered. She came on to me, by the way, not the other way around. I wasn't looking for a girlfriend. She's not even my type, not that I have a type exactly, I just mean that I don't remember being attracted to her.

I don't even remember the first time we met. She says it was at the gallery when I was dropping off the piece for Nomi's show, the one from my magnified grubworm series, which I still think is one of my best. I know she was working there then but I don't remember meeting her. She was one of those nice efficient girls who don't make much of an impression, who are always just around taking care of business. She wasn't bad looking. She had a nice little body, short dark hair, big brown eyes, but she was bland somehow, a little too wholesome. Or maybe I just didn't notice her because I was so crazy about Val in those days, Big Valley I used to call her. Roxanne must have been at the opening too although I don't remember that either. I was probably with Val who probably had her hands down my pants and we were probably high, as usual.

Things blew up pretty soon after that. Val, school, my job, my little brush with the law. I had to get out of town. I went to Seattle and when that got old, L.A., then I ran out of money and went to Phoenix to stay with my parents and when they kicked me out I went to Austin where Val was by then, dancing in some strip bar with her hair dyed magenta. I don't remember much else about that year except for waking up in rehab, back in Phoenix, with a broken nose. By the time I got back to Chicago, to finish grad school, all the teachers had decided I was an asshole so I quit. They had to admit I could draw though. Anyway, the next time I saw Roxanne was sometime after that.

That I remember. For one thing I was clean and sober. I'd just gotten back into town and I was making the rounds of the galleries with my new work. I don't know why I even went into Lee Hastings's. I knew the guy hated the kind of work I was doing—*pseudo-intellectual derivative artsy-craftsy bullshit* I believe was the technical term he used to describe it. I guess I thought because I'd had that one piece in the group show there two years before it gave me an in but I was wrong even though my new work was completely different.

By that time I was making these little boxes with drawers in them, covering them with cut-out pictures from old encyclopedias and maps and pages from old math and biology textbooks I found at flea markets. I'd draw simple objects on top of the pictures and then put the real objects into the drawers—butterflies, twigs, empty pill bottles, that kind of stuff. Some of it gave off a little smell. It was kind of science project-y with more than a whiff of Joseph Cornell, I admit. But so what? I'd grown up on the Cornell boxes at the Art Institute. They were the high point of every field trip I took as a kid, them and the naked ladies of course and the mummies at the Field Museum. What's wrong with being influenced by a master? When they like you they call it appropriation, when they don't they say it's derivative. Fuck 'em all.

I was working on this idea of how you know something. Do you have to go to school and memorize it and categorize it and store the knowledge in books and little airtight drawers? Or can you just take it in and let it go, like breathing?

I was going door-to-door, gallery-to-gallery, and figured what the hell. And there she was, this vaguely familiar same brown-haired girl in the same chair at the same front desk except she looked different now, older, more loosely put together, not so tight and smiley. Better. She was wearing a black V-neck sweater over an open-necked white blouse and a pink lace push-up bra I could just see the top of. I smiled at her and walked right past, straight to Lee's office in back.

Lee took one look at my work and basically kicked me out. It was embarrassing. I had to walk all the way back past Roxanne to get out of the place. To save face, I suppose, I handed her my card. I didn't mean anything by it. But five minutes later she left a message on my phone.

It was her idea to have lunch. We met the next day at Good Gravy, one of those fashionable little fake diners down the street from the gallery, and sat in a turquoise vinyl booth. She slid down with her back to the door in case Lee came in. Before the menus even arrived she'd told me about her divorce and her kid—I hadn't known she was married and couldn't have cared less—and suggested some new galleries that had opened since I'd left town that might be interested in what I was doing. She made a list on the paper placemat and drew a map showing where each one was. I told her the whole story about Val and Austin and rehab and grad school and the overdose and said I'd been playing with a band called Golgotha since I got back and that's when she got excited. She sat up straight and drew in a little breath and actually blushed—I couldn't think of the last time I'd seen a girl do that—and said *you don't meet many Christians in this line of work.*

I have to say it was striking. I'd assumed that because she was so straight-looking she wasn't very interesting. I was impressed she even knew what Golgotha was. Tim named it, I didn't, and it's not really a good name for a Christian band. All most people hear is Goth. I tried to explain I just played with them sometimes. I did try to tell her. I said I wasn't really a hardcore believer, or only sort of, recently, since rehab, but I don't think she heard any of it. She was too excited telling me about how she'd just gone back to *The Church* as she called it and how happy it made her and how hollow all this—she waved her hand toward the window indicating the galleries I suppose—seemed by comparison. Then she invited me to her church.

Honestly, I thought she was just being nice. I certainly didn't have any designs on her. She was cute, sure, but she'd just gone through a divorce and she had a little kid and I was just getting clean and not looking to start anything. And frankly she wasn't that cute. I mean she was attractive but she wasn't even the prettiest girl, sorry, woman, I'd had lunch with that week. And she was no girl, either. She was five years older than me. That sounds bad, I know, like I'm sexist, like I don't respect women—and I do, I respect the hell out of them contrary to what you all may have heard—but all I mean is—let's be frank—she wasn't irresistible. She wasn't worth breaking my vow for, the vow of celibacy I'd made in group when I got clean two months before.

They have you make a pledge. Six months was the deal you were expected to agree to. No entanglements, no sex, no dating even, for six whole months. They couldn't enforce it, of course. It was a promise, and the big idea was you came out of rehab being someone who could keep a promise.

It may sound strange but I welcomed it. Not the no-sex part exactly though I didn't even mind that, but mostly I welcomed permission to say no. To women. To sex. To all of it. It gave me permission to not have a girlfriend. I was twenty-nine years old and I hadn't gone six months without a girlfriend since I was fifteen. I looked forward to it, to the chance to clear my head. I thought it would be good for my work.

She ordered a Greek salad and iced tea and I ordered the cheeseburger plate with everything and when the mustard slid out of the bun and down my chin and onto my shirt she stuck her napkin in my 7UP and dabbed the mustard off, smiling in a way that should have alarmed me if I'd been paying attention, if I hadn't been so flattered by what she was saying about my work. It wasn't just the presumption of touch, motherly though it was, that seemed a little off even then. It was the way she seemed to like the mess I'd made, the way she was showing me she was going to clean it up whether I wanted her to or not. I should have noticed, I should have suddenly remembered an appointment and slapped a twenty on the table and gotten out of there right then, as fast as I could. Instead, when the check came, she took it and I let her. "I'm the one with a job," she said, brushing up against me as we walked out the door.

So that Saturday night I picked them up, Roxanne and her kid, April, and we all went to church. It was one of those places with extra services Saturday night meant to appeal to *singles*— God, I hate that word, it reminds me of American cheese—one of those places with video screens and a sanctuary the size of a basketball stadium. She'd told me that one of the assistant pastors was a friend of hers and said she thought maybe he could get Golgotha a gig there. We looked for him after the service but we didn't see him so she said she'd leave him a message and then she asked if I wanted to come back to her house for tea and I felt like I owed her something so I went.

Look, it was innocent, or not even that. It was an obligation. I didn't expect danger because I wasn't attracted to her. Besides, April was there. And I'd already told her I couldn't drink. I'd even told her about my vow. So we made popcorn and put April to bed—I could already see she was a great kid—and after that we sat on the couch with Mr. Cosmo and talked about art and then I went home.

For a while it was all nice and platonic. And it was good for my work. In those days she was interested in hearing about it. During the week I worked on my boxes and on Saturday night we all went to church and after that we went back to her house and drank tea. After a few weeks I started going to her fellowship group on Wednesday night and afterward we'd go to her house and drink more tea. Sometimes she had a glass of wine and I said go ahead I'm not even tempted although I was.

She had this house in the suburbs, this big empty barn of a place she got in the divorce settlement and there was this lifetime supply of temperature-controlled wine there that the guy had just left behind. The kitchen was like something out of a movie and some nights I cooked dinner—it was preemptive, she was a lousy cook—and when she went to check on April I'd do a little wine tasting and some nights I even stayed on a mattress in the guest room so I wouldn't have to drive all the way back to the city and then back out to the suburbs again the next morning where I taught a Tuesday Thursday section of Intro to Drawing at Lake County Community College.

On those mornings, after spending the night in the guest room, I made omelets, and French toast for April, and before we ate breakfast April said grace. Sometimes, while we waited for Jack to come babysit, April did little tricks. She could recite the books of the Bible in backwards order. It was nice—that's all. We were friends playing house.

Then one Saturday night April wasn't there when I showed up to take them to church—Roxanne said her ex's parents had taken April to Disney World for the weekend—so after church we went back to the house alone. There we were, sitting on the couch in front of this huge remote-controlled gas fireplace, me drinking this noxious herbal tea as usual and her with a glass of wine, when she said I looked tired and offered to give me a back rub. OK, I said. The next thing I knew she'd stripped down to her purple lace bra and was sitting on my back.

Afterward she said I shouldn't worry because the moratorium on sex didn't count if you were in love. I said wait a minute. How do you know? And who said anything about love? Then she started to cry and that's how it started. I hate to disappoint people. Although, I'm told, I usually do.

26

I felt bad about breaking my vow. *Just say no* they told us in rehab. We all laughed about that. It's easier said than done, especially to Roxanne. Roxanne was so intense about everything right from the start. I felt guilty saying no to her. It got to the point where I felt guiltier for not having sex with her—once when I tried to put my pants back on she threw a kitchen timer at my head and said I was being selfish—than I felt when I did have sex with her. Can you understand? Everything happened before I had a chance to think. Or choose. *That's how it's supposed to be you fucking moron* Roxanne said when I told her that, when I said I thought I just needed to back off a little, needed a chance to think. She said you're not supposed to think you're supposed to feel, that's what life is.

And I tried to, feel that is, I really did, but honestly all I felt was kind of numb and I was torn between what I'd promised in group and what Roxanne made me promise and I never got the chance to choose anything. *It's meant to be*, she said. *Can't you tell?* I was afraid to say it, but the truth was, I couldn't.

I don't mean I didn't love her. I didn't mean to say that. I mean that I didn't want to love her. Of course I loved her. Don't even ask. How could you not love Roxanne? She's a good person. Everybody loves Roxanne. The guys in the band were crazy about her, they'd come over all the time and she'd order pizza and we'd all hang out in the kitchen. She liked being the only girl. They all thought she was great. I'm the bad one here, apparently. And then there was April. She was so little then. Whenever I tried to break it off I thought of her and I couldn't leave. Not that she didn't already have a father; she did. Drake's a good guy. It's just that he lived in Connecticut half the time and it seemed like she needed fifty fathers, one in every state. That part, April, was OK. I knew it was a package deal and I didn't mind. I even liked the idea of being a father, or a sort of part-time stepfather, in the abstract at least, but I needed time to think.

By then I was living with Roxanne pretty much full time, not officially but just de facto, and finally I said, look. I need some time off to think and she said *fine, go then*, and flung a spatula in the direction of my crotch.

Before I left I changed all the burned-out light bulbs and made a fresh pot of sweet potato soup. *This is supposed to make it all right?* she said, tilting the pot over the garbage disposal as I piled my stuff at the back door. *Please don't throw it out*, I said. *April likes it.*

We agreed not to talk for a month. I made it sound like I was leaving town for a while and at first I did. I drove all day and all night to Austin and stayed there for four days but Val was less than pleased to see me and it didn't work out with Lonnie, either, this other girl I went to see, so after sleeping in my car for three nights in the parking lot at the Broken Spoke I ended up driving back to Chicago, to my apartment.

I slept for two days. Then I went out and bought groceries. Cleaned up my studio. Stayed sober, stayed home, cooked—I was working on replicating a perfect chicken fried steak I'd eaten somewhere outside Nacogdoches—and worked on my boxes. It felt good. I felt good. I duct taped cardboard over the windows and hoped Roxanne wouldn't see the light if she drove through the alley at night. I was back to being celibate. I figured I still owed myself three and a half months.

My work had never gone better. For the first time in years I felt like I was making a real breakthrough. That's when I started drawing on road maps. Actually the road maps had been Roxanne's idea. Then one night the phone rang while I was in the bathtub having a smoke and I heard Roxanne's voice on the answering machine—she sounded hoarse—saying the word *pregnant.*

Mr. Cosmo

I felt terribly nervous in the weeks before May's arrival. I don't mean to sound self-absorbed although I know that's how people think of me—flighty and selfish and handsome—but the stress in that household was almost unbearable by then. I just wanted a little peace, can you blame me? I couldn't eat, not really, just a little rice and yogurt sometimes and then I'd still throw up and my hair started to fall out. And I've always been a fitful sleeper. But with Roxanne crying all the time and Craig never home and then when he was Roxanne following him around screaming at him and April in her most excitable state—well, I'm more empathetic than people realize and I couldn't help but feel everyone's feelings. I started having fits.

Then the day Roxanne brought May home I could feel something terrible coming. I had to leave.

They arrived by cab. Greasy-haired Roxanne, her face wet with tears, clutching that dark baby to her chest like her life depended on it and standing at the curb with bags hanging off her shoulders and off her elbows and around her neck while the cabbie unloaded more from the trunk. I could see it all from the picture window behind the couch where I'd been waiting. The cabbie carried everything to the door and she came in crying, holding that baby who was perfectly silent. "Hello, Mr. Cosmo," she said, but there was no kiss and after that she completely ignored me, turned her back on me to dig something out of one of her bags, and when she did there it was, that little brown face looking over her shoulder just staring down at me. We exchanged thoughts. *Welcome and good luck*, I said, not too bitterly I hope. *I hope you enjoy your stay.*

A while later Craig drove up with April in the back—I could see her wailing in profile through the window, poor thing, her little mouth drawn down like the sad half of a harlequin mask, disappointed I suppose to have missed the big arrival or having a low blood sugar episode or suffering from who knows what other tragedy or just in sympathy with the generally sorry state of affairs in the house. April was always upset about something. Inside, Roxanne, with perfect dramatic timing and in full view of the door through which Craig was about to make his entrance, was sobbing as she changed the baby's diaper on the kitchen table.

Craig parked the car, got out, slammed the door, opened the door in the back, lifted April carefully from her little chair, hoisted her onto his hip and smoothed her hair. She wrapped her legs around his waist and draped her arms limply about his neck still wearing that open-mouthed expression which suggested more the memory of crying and readiness for more than crying itself and then he slammed the back car door shut and opened the trunk and with one hand took out a cellophane-wrapped bouquet of suffocated flowers, a teddy bear with a smudged bow around its neck, an enormous package of diapers and a box of cheap cigars—I could smell them all the way inside the house. Then he slammed the trunk shut.

He moved heavily, with what I think of now as a sense of doom. As he came inside, shouldering the door open and trying to get the diapers through without banging April's head or crushing the already ruined flowers or dropping the teddy bear, I slipped out past him, not wanting to hear what surely would come next, and left for Bill and Phoebe's, for a stay of indeterminate length.

PHOEBE

I'm sitting in the back of the cave, holding a long stick with a puppet on the end. I jiggle the puppet at the mouth of the cave, which is cleverly disguised to resemble a suburban front porch. Passersby smile and wave at me, at the puppet me that is, and I wave my little puppet hand back. The puppet me smiles incessantly. I can't help it, the smile is painted on. The passersby, charmed by my effervescent conversation—I am a ventriloquist too—and endlessly cheerful nature, invite me to come out with them, to their houses for dinner, to their country clubs and summer homes for sailboat rides and leisurely breakfasts of poached eggs and smoked trout on the deck, chilled white wine and theater in the barn when it gets dark. Such a charming guest I'd make, they think—little do they know—but I can't leave my cave of course and I can't tell them why. Sometimes the puppet oversteps and accepts their invitations and then I have to invent excuses and send my regrets. It's awkward but I'm always forgiven. Charm like mine, like the puppet's I mean, goes a long way. Later they bring me food and souvenirs from their travels and lay them on the welcome mat with notes that say *we hope you'll join us next time!*

I am a good neighbor, well-liked, a well-liked puppet. It's a good thing they don't know the real me, back in here squatting in the dust and peeing in the dirt, picking cold burned potatoes from the ashes of a burned-out fire with my long filthy fingernails, smashing bats against the wall with a stick. My blindfold bites into my face and makes me sweat. Even if I took it off it would be too dark to see.

My therapist, Lois, says I'm being dramatic. *Don't obfuscate,* she says. *Enough with the literary devices.* She is emotionless and stern but with just a twinkle to let me know she appreciates my efforts to amuse her, not knowing I mean it literally. Not knowing that the puppet me is talking right now, that the tether that keeps me tied to the cave has been let out far enough to let me come all this way to see her and that it is the puppet that is talking to her in this charming simulation of insight and self-deprecating wit and impressive comprehension of the latest psychoanalytic terms. *OK then* I say in her language. *Another way to put it is to say that I don't like to leave the house.* We are discussing why I wasn't at the airport with flowers to meet Roxanne when she came back with the baby.

I feel bad about it. Guilty. I'm not so out of it that I don't know there should have been a welcoming party. There was supposed to be, but Roxanne had to change her flight and the email didn't go out until the last minute and when she called Craig he had his phone off and his fly down and Jack doesn't have a cell phone and never picks up messages anyway and when Roxanne called me I didn't answer either. I hate the phone. Finally, no one showed up.

I hate crowds, hate airports and am not wildly fond of babies but if I'd known nobody else was going to be there, I would have made an exception. I would have taken a pill and gone. I am allowed off my leash I mean I do venture out for certain occasions, and I can collect myself in an emergency when I need to, which is what this surely was, given Roxanne's nature. But I had no idea.

You notice I do not say that I am incapable of leaving the cave, only that I strongly prefer not to when other people are present. I haven't always been like this. I used to go out, used to like to go out even. I used to wash my hair every day. I thought nothing of meeting Duane in the city for dinner, dressing up in a tight skirt and thigh highs and no underwear, back when I was seventy pounds lighter, putting on bracelets, earrings, mascara and an off-the-shoulder shawl to go eat overpriced pasta somewhere, and maybe check into a hotel afterward where we'd undress in front of the window and imagine who was watching.

I liked hotels in those days. We'd do things in bed with food that were too messy to do at home. Room service made everything possible. I never dreamt I'd stop doing these things, never thought I'd stop wanting to. I was in my thirties then, I thought life would go on forever like that, that there would always be enough of everything—enough time enough money enough love enough sex enough beauty enough collagen enough hair enough desire. Enough Duane.

The puppet was always there for emergencies, of course, in my purse or in my pocket or in my makeup case—she's collapsible and almost weightless, like freeze-dried food, just add panic and she pops into shape—but in those days I controlled her, not the other way around. I never thought twice about going out of the house in those days, talking to strangers, riding in elevators, standing in lines at public toilets even, at all those ballgames Duane loved so much. It seemed, at the risk of sounding fatuous, fun.

I even used to enjoy travel. I used to enjoy that transparently false yet thrilling sense of enlarged possibility I got from boarding a plane in one city and getting off in another. I used to enjoy that illusion of instant transformation, cheap though it was. I liked the feeling of shrugging off the old self and slipping into the new one as if into an orange ball gown in some underlit dressing room of an out-of-town thrift shop while thinking this time it will fit and that fact alone will change everything.

I used to love the surprise as I debarked from the plane or the train or the boat or the taxi in a new locale. I loved the bracing, spicy whiff of a new land and the new life it promised, if only for eighteen days. There was always some detail you forgot to expect. Humidity—how novel! Palm trees—how picturesque! Heat—well I never! Markets! Cathedrals! The smell of snow in summer! Those darling pastries being cooked on a cart in the open air! What are those spices in the potatoes? The bracing spillage of unfamiliar consonants clanging together as if in a metal pot! The jazz band on the steps of the Louvre! Greasy fish and chips wrapped in newspaper at two in the morning! The bugs in the Russian hotel bed! Pink money! The man with crooked teeth selling poems on the street in Rotterdam! Selling them!

I never thought about planes crashing into buildings, immolation in the lavatory, decapitation at the ferryboat landing, parasites in the sushi. I remember when surprise was delicious, not terrifying.

Just remembering makes me wistful, not for going but for wanting to. Duane and I traveled the world, planning our trips at the kitchen table, checking out library books on native foods weeks in advance, practicing recipes to get in the mood. We borrowed language tapes and, failing at that, spoke in foreign accents to each other as we got drunk on the local wines and beers of our next destination. I was on a longer leash in those days. I could go for weeks and never even feel it tug. I might still be let off for a kind of sabbatical—a puppet's week off as it were—if it weren't for that vexing problem of the people you meet once you get there, the necessity of making conversation, of accounting for oneself. I am here because . . . At home I am . . . My husband is . . . That's when I get nervous. Even the puppet ran out of things to say and after that it was easier just to stay home.

Mostly now I leave the house only when I don't expect to see anyone. I arranged to work at home. I tried to go to the office for a while, after all this started, but the puppet took over and made a mess of it. She was always agreeing to things I couldn't possibly do, always nodding and smiling, so pathetically trying to fit in, to please. She agreed to go out for drinks after work, volunteered to head up a productivity committee, once she even offered to organize a morale-building outing to a bowling alley. I had to put a stop to it when my boss complained I had *bad follow-through skills.*

Now I just stay home. Email and FedEx make it possible and, except for the excruciating monthly staff meeting I am required to attend, a compromise I agreed to along with a pay cut so that I could spend the other nineteen workdays of the month at home, I do not go into the office. I do not go in for my so-called performance review—they can write whatever they please so long as they don't make me sit through its recitation—or for the departmental volley ball games or the bonus day pep talks or the baby showers or the Christmas raffle or the going-away pizza parties for disgraced department heads.

On the rare occasion that someone insists on meeting in person they come here. The puppet is quite hospitable. Of course we prepare. I order in appropriate refreshments, coffee, juice and sweet rolls for morning meetings, cookies and fruit in the afternoon. I move the stacks of newspapers close to the wall to look as though they're waiting to be recycled. I hire a cleaning service to come early in the morning on the day of the meeting to spruce up the kitchen and the bathroom and remove dog hair and all other signs of my personality from any part of the house a visitor might see. I polish up the puppet. I even get dressed.

I know there's a lovely if somewhat judgmental compound Greek word for this preference of mine, a word that Lois likes to bandy about sometimes in her more pompous moments, but it's not exactly fair to say that I'm afraid to leave the house, just that I am disinclined to do so. It's better to say I lead a quiet life, to say that I keep to myself. The Internet makes it possible. Google has saved me from the noisy new democracy of the library, thank God. I order my clothes from L.L. Bean, my books from Amazon, my food from Peapod, my kibble and treats from Drs. Foster and Smith. And that's enough. The marketplace no longer interests me. Who was that Greek—I could Google him in a under a minute—who ventured out to the agora after a long seclusion only to observe that it satisfied him to see all that he did not want? The one whose name means dog in Greek? That's me.

Though in truth I do go out, if against my better judgment. I walk the dogs every day. I walk them early in the morning and then again late at night and I let them into the yard at other times. I see people. The puppet is more than polite. I say hello to the FedEx girl. I even know her name. It's Gayle. I know because she sent me a Christmas card. I go into the world for necessities. I keep my car in good order, Duane's nineteen-year-old Volvo, Dolly, which is the same age as the child we might have had if we'd gone ahead and had one the last time we discussed it. I take her to the mechanic twice a year, more if something goes wrong. I stay on top of things. I take the dogs to the vet at the first sign of trouble and once a year to update their shots. Sometimes I even shop, at night usually. I stock up on lined index cards, yellow tablets and the soft pencils I crave at the big-box office supply store, which stays open until ten. That I have to nap after these exhausting social encounters is my own business.

I say I walk my dogs but I only have Bill full time now. Sweet Helene, who showed up in my garage six years ago, cold, collarless and already gray around the muzzle, died in her sleep last August, all bones and surrender. That's why I don't mind Mr. Cosmo's visits. He livens up the place. Bill used to do that, liven things up, but sensitive Bill is older and more subdued now. He seems to have taken on my sorrows as his own and I'm afraid I've dampened his high spirits with my gloom. I even used to have a cat, a reddish orange tabby named Fellini. He was Duane's and he livened things up plenty when he was here, dragging chipmunks onto the porch to kill and eat, leaving decapitated mice in the hall for me to step on when I got up at night to go to the bathroom. He slunk off though, after Duane died, looking for more witty company than mine I suppose. I miss him but I don't blame him—things were no fun anymore with Duane gone. So I welcomed Mr. Cosmo. It took a dog that obliviously self-absorbed, with his fits and his foibles and his insulating cloud of stink, to liven up this house.

A few words about Mr. Cosmo are in order here. He's a pure-bred, you might say over-bred, Weimaraner, a silvery moody dog with three-and-a-half legs, pale pink-rimmed eyes, a pink belly and a varying number of supernumerary nipples that swell up sometimes and make him appear to be female and pregnant. He has some kind of glandular problem Roxanne claims to be treating with herbs. I imagine his missing half-leg is a casualty of puppy exuberance, of dashing through an unlatched gate in front of a car though nobody knows for sure—it was already gone when Roxanne adopted him—and its absence doesn't seem to bother him at all. He hops.

I don't usually care for purebred dogs but Mr. Cosmo is such a mess, such an extravagant example of bad breeding, that I've made an exception for him, especially since he has a beautiful smile when he's not throwing up and because he is remarkably prone to eye contact. He often escapes from Roxanne's yard to visit me and will sit for hours at my side while I work or read, attempting to catch my eye and hold it as long as he can. When I can stand his gaze no longer I'll put him and Bill in the yard and now and then he'll figure out a way to leave, despite my expensive fence, to take himself for a walk. On these occasions I curse him when I'm forced to go searching for him in broad daylight, but when I see him down the street hopping along with that endearing lopsided purposeful gait that makes him look like a drunk about town my heart seizes. His will to explore the world is so trusting, his nature so open and so opposite mine that despite his demands, his moods and allergies, his awkward and malodorous body, I've come to find him quite dear.

He found me. He showed up at my front door one day. Bill, ordinarily a calm, even stoic, dog, stood in the hall pointing his whole body toward the door, and barked. When I opened it there was Mr. Cosmo, sitting calmly on the welcome mat, staring into my eyes and smiling like a Mormon evangelist. What could I do but invite him inside. I kept him three days before I called the number on his tag, to punish the negligent fool who'd let him roam, and when I finally called her Roxanne thanked me but hardly seemed to notice he'd been gone. She said she'd pick him up later. *Later.*

At first I loathed her on principle, assuming only a negligent fool would let a three-and-a-half legged dog go off on his own and not worry, assuming it was her fault he was missing half a leg to begin with. But then as he visited more often I got to know them, Roxanne and Mr. Cosmo both, and I saw how it went. I could see that his need to wander was no reflection on her or anyone's efforts to keep him at home or for that matter on his attachment to her or later to me. He simply liked to go off by himself and was brilliant at escape. I came to admire his ingenuity and independence, not to mention Roxanne's willingness to adopt and keep a three-legged wandering dog, and eventually we all became friends, at least to the extent I was able.

Though you couldn't just be friends, if that's what you'd call what we were, with Roxanne. She traveled in a pack and you never knew who else might show up with her or instead of her when she said she'd come over to drop off Mr. Cosmo, and maybe it was her distracted nature that allowed me to allow her to befriend me at all. She couldn't concentrate on me long enough to remember my lapses. In those days that was just right.

The first member of Roxanne's pack I met was her mother. *Just call me Jack* she'd said in that gravelly contralto of hers, hitching up the waistband of her baggy polyester khakis as she flicked ashes companionably onto my shoe. She was one of those boiled-looking little women who bought her clothes in the boys department at Sears and who, with her putty-like skin, short spiky gray hair, knobby spotted hands and filthy child-sized gym shoes, appeared both ageless and sexless. The fact that she'd borne Roxanne seemed like an anomaly, some odd one-time event, like something you'd read about one of those fish that changes gender midway through life. I liked her right away. Those piercing black brown eyes, though, were too much for me. I had to like her at a distance.

The next week I met April. She and Jack had come by early in the morning to drop off Mr. Cosmo. Roxanne was getting ready to host a *gratitude brunch* for some church group of hers and needed the weekend to prepare. Even then, at four, April stood out as a savant of social poise. It was partly how she looked. With that backlit halo of glowing white blonde hair, standing there on the porch in her Capri-length blue jeans and orange tennis shoes, holding Jack's hand on one side and Mr.

Cosmo's leash on the other, she shone like some medieval angel, especially between those two gray gargoyles.

And it wasn't only how she looked. When Jack introduced her she held out her pale little hand and said, *I'm pleased to meet you, Phoebe*, carefully over-enunciating to compensate for the slight sibilance created by a missing front tooth. Even the puppet was too shocked to reply. It didn't occur to me until later to wonder how she knew my first name. Jack had introduced me as Mrs. Patience.

Not long after that, on yet another dog exchange, I met Drake—nice guy, and nice-looking—and his parents, Drake Sr. and Elizabeth, in whose bony leathery face I could see the origins of later generations of good looks. April had inherited her hot blue eyes.

Elizabeth I recognized. I'd known women like her all my life, women who felt superior to people like me and Roxanne and Jack, better. Richer, thinner, tanner, more mannerly, better groomed, more active on charitable boards and, when all else failed, simply taller. You could tell someone in her family, though not her and not recently, had once made a great deal of money.

Being better was tiring, you could tell. Elizabeth's face looked wrung out, a result maybe of all those years of grimacing in a pretend smile, trying to contain her revulsion for the likes of us, years of being affronted by others' faux pas and bad smells at charity events when all she wanted was to go home and pour herself a glass of gin. All that trying not to say what she thought, having to catch the mean words between her tongue and her teeth before they slipped out, had taken its toll. Though I knew she didn't like me, I felt a little sorry for her.

In particular Roxanne's presence seemed to weigh on her. Elizabeth had to negotiate with her whenever she wanted access to April and I could see at a glance how hard the necessary politeness was. Her effort to restrain herself from correcting Roxanne's every move tortured her face even while it glowed with expensive moisturizing cosmetics. I could see from the way she twisted her hands together the memory of all those times she'd tried to keep from twitching Roxanne's napkin into place, adding more to the tip behind her back.

Roxanne was oblivious to Elizabeth's disapproval, as she seemed to be to most of the dangers in her life, or pretended to be. *Poor old dehydrated witch* is what she called her, or sometimes just *the tower of power*, cheerfully chucking Elizabeth's annual holiday gift of a pastel cashmere sweater set into the Goodwill bag.

To complete the list of Roxanne's circle, there was also April's box turtle Magellan, who had a surprisingly large personality for a turtle and who I watched, along with Mr. Cosmo, when they all went on trips. Then later there was less of Drake and his parents and a lot more of Pastor Gary, who pretended to smile at me while he looked right past me. I used to call him, in my head of course, back when I had secret names for everyone, Pasteurized Gary. It's not that funny, I know, but I couldn't help it. I'd picked up the habit from my father. My therapist Lois disapproves of this hobby of mine. She says it's a distancing mechanism and in a rare show of moral indignation once said she thought it was a little mean and reminded her of exactly what I said I didn't like about Elizabeth. The puppet replied to this criticism by nodding and saying she didn't doubt for a minute that Lois was absolutely right. I didn't say I thought her real objection was that she suspected me of having a secret name for her. Which in fact I do although I think she would agree, if I told her what it is, which I would never do, that it is not especially mean.

Then there was Craig. I wondered if I should warn Roxanne, but what was the point. And finally came May, beautiful May, who would split my heart open with her silence and who, I will always regret, arrived that day at the airport to a welcoming party of none.

Mr. Cosmo and Bill have gotten along since the day they met, even though they're opposites or maybe because they are. Bill is some kind of mix Duane and I picked out at the shelter, too big and black and mangy, in those days, to easily attract a home. *Give us one you'd otherwise kill*, Duane had said, getting to the point, making me blanch, and out came Bill, covered with scabs. Once starved and neglected and formerly seventy-nine pounds, he now weighs one hundred twelve and ought to be on a diet. He's as housebound as Mr. Cosmo is flighty. Stable, steady, big, black and solid, he wouldn't leave me for ten thousand meatballs let alone a walk down the block. The only bad thing I can think of to say about him is that he, who once was bald, now sheds like a demon. They told me at the shelter they thought he was a Great Pyrenees Labrador Retriever mix maybe with some Newfoundland and German shepherd mixed in and with his bulky body, long black silky coat and intelligent carmelly eyes I guess I can see any and all of those breeds in him. Not that I care.

When people at the dog park inquired what breed Bill was Duane used to make things up. He's a Himalayan truffle hound, he'd say, patting Bill's head proudly and smiling that dazzling smile of his. Or he'd tell them Bill was a French kitchen dog or a rare Chien de Bofinger, or a Giant Box Turtle Terrier bred to out-swim and capture special soup turtles. People would just smile and nod. Those were the days, when everything was funny.

ROXANNE

Everybody thinks it's all my fault and I suppose that most of it is. Though I don't know what else I should have done. I got pregnant, yes, but that takes two. I didn't prevent it—neither did he—but I didn't exactly plan it either. The Lord works in mysterious ways and sometimes He doesn't mind a little help. Craig knew what might happen. He knew how I felt about abortion.

At first he was upset. He accused me of arranging it, tricking him, trapping him. Railroading him, he said. He even accused me of making it up but I didn't care what he said. By then it didn't matter what he thought. Time would tell. A baby was on the way and he was the father whether he liked it or not. As Pastor Gary said, it was time for him to man up.

Before I told him, before I knew for sure, we split up. He went away for a while and I let him. I could have told him then I thought I was pregnant, I could have stopped him, but I let him go. I figured I'd let the Lord call the shots, let things happen the way they were supposed to instead of trying to force it. If he was meant to come back, he would. If I was meant to have his baby, I would.

I don't know where he went. I never asked. I willed myself not to care. Maybe to Phoenix to sponge off his parents but probably back to Austin, on a binge. Back to Val, I suppose. But I don't know and I almost don't care. I don't care. What happened when we were apart doesn't matter. I knew he'd come back eventually, when he found out he was going to be a father, if he was going to be. Then I found out for sure and I tried to wait but I weakened. I called and left a message, telling him the news.

He showed up here the next night. Just showed up in the rain looking like he'd been up all night and I let him in and we sat at the kitchen table and talked. We were quiet, we didn't even turn on the lights, so as not to wake up April. I told him I was having the baby with him or without him and that whether he liked it or not he'd always be her father—I could tell it was a girl—so did he want to know his child or not.

At first he got mad—quiet, I said, April's asleep—and then he cried and then we prayed together and then he said well OK then. He said he wanted to do the right thing, that it was in God's hands now, and I said the God part's over, buddy, now it's in your hands, and he said all right then, he wanted to do what God wanted him to do, and it seemed like this was what God had planned for him so he wanted it. Let go and let God, he said. One day at a time. Then he went off to sleep on his old mattress in the guest room.

It wasn't the homecoming I'd hoped for but I knew he'd come around. Or not even come around but see that he loved me, that he always had and that he loved the baby too and wanted the baby because he was a good man and he was ready to settle down even if he didn't realize it. I told him that. I said I know that underneath all this childish behavior and bad boy bullshit you're a good man and you want this and will do right by this baby girl who needs a strong man to be her daddy. I told him I know you will get a real job and help to support her since Drake's child support only goes so far and even though his parents are very generous that money is intended for April and I don't want this baby to feel poor. And, I reminded him, Drake's parents paid for the house but I pay the real estate taxes and they are ungodly.

Sometimes I think now I should have let him go that night when he wanted to and saved us all a lot of pain. But it's too late now. Besides, if I had, I wouldn't have May.

So we got married. Three weeks later. It was a simple ceremony, which is what I wanted after the embarrassing circus I'd had the first time—the hand-lettered invitations, the fourteen attendants, the country club dinner for 182 guests, the wedding cake-shaped dress, the four bridal showers, the ridiculous trous-seau, the eight-piece band, the seven-tiered cake, the china pat-tern-picking outing with Drake's mother, the fights with my own mother over what she'd wear—absolutely no gym shoes not even if they're new I'd had to tell her. All that work and look how that turned out. Drake's parents paid for everything, but it cost me a year of my life, two if you count the thank you notes, which I never even finished. There was no way I'd go through that again.

We had the wedding at home on a Saturday morning. I wore a cream-colored linen maternity suit and ballet flats. Craig wore a pink bow tie and red cowboy boots. We agreed to write our own vows although later I found out Craig got Tim to write his in exchange for a bag of pot.

Nineteen people came, including the neighbors. Gary mar-ried us. My childhood friend Ruth and my mother were the witnesses—Craig told everyone my mother was his best man. Craig's parents and grandmother flew in from Phoenix the day before and his sister sent regrets and a wooden salad bowl. Later I found out she hadn't spoken to Craig in six years but nobody would tell me why. Craig claimed not to remember.

Ruth flew in early from Atlanta to help me get ready. I'd tracked her down when I went back to church—she'd never left—and we'd been close ever since. Now she was a soloist in her church choir and she offered to sing at the wedding, as a gift.

When she'd offered, over the phone, I'd said thank you, of course. What else could I say? But it turned into kind of a problem. I didn't expect Craig to have such strong feelings about the music and they had a little tiff two nights before the wed-ding. We were having dinner when she said she planned to sing that Dan Fogelberg song, the one about fishes in the ocean that everybody uses. Craig said he thought he was going to be sick and then he said he couldn't go through with it if she was going to sing that f-ing song and she was insulted of course although I wish she would have at least noticed he made the effort to say *f-ing* out of deference for her religious views. To spite him

I think she offered to sing a hymn instead—"By Vows of Love Together Bound"—which, she said, she knew by heart because she'd just sung it at someone else's wedding. That made him even madder and he slammed his knife and fork down on the kitchen table and walked out of the room.

I had no idea he cared so much. I thought it was kind of sweet. Though later I realized he was just embarrassed. His band would be there and he didn't want them to think he had bad taste. After I calmed him down he came back to the table and we brainstormed a list of songs. Ruth almost had him talked into "What a Wonderful World" but Craig said it wasn't that great a song except when Louis Armstrong sang it and we finally agreed on the Beatles. "In My Life." Ruth has a beautiful voice and I thought it sounded fine, but I saw Craig wince during the melisma at the end, on *more*. Golgotha played an acoustic set of their own songs later.

After the short ceremony—and I mean short—we had brunch. That was nice. Phoebe had sent a case of something expensive the week before when I told her the news though of course neither Craig nor I could drink. Craig handled all the food—including a lemon cheesecake he made from scratch. Everyone said it was incredible, though I was too sick to eat a thing.

Phoebe came late—I was worried she might not show up at all—dressed in a black tent covered in dog hair. I didn't take it personally, the vampire get-up or the dog hair. That's just Phoebe. She stood by the door the whole time, guzzling champagne and eating deviled eggs, in case, she said, she had an attack of claustrophobia and had to leave. She brought Bill to steady her nerves. She'd shampooed him for the occasion but he still shed all over everything including my suit. There were three dogs there, which made Craig's parents nervously hold their plates close to their chests but which I thought of as good luck. There was Mr. Cosmo, of course, coughing up capers and begging for cheesecake, the freshly shampooed Bill, and the neighbors' cockapoo Perry who had to be taken home when the band

45

started to play because the noise hurt his ears and he started to cry.

There was no honeymoon.

Three days later I had the miscarriage. I woke up from an afternoon nap feeling like I was getting my period and drove myself straight to the hospital—who knows where Craig was—and by dinnertime the baby was gone, dead. As I'd expected, it was a girl. I named her Patricia Jaclyn, after Craig's mother, and mine.

Afterward, my mother came to stay for a while, to take care of April. She slept on the couch and Craig moved back to the guest room. We didn't discuss it, he just went.

Except to go to the bathroom and occasionally shower, I didn't get out of bed for a month. After two months I still hadn't left the house and it was six before I began to feel normal again. I don't mean physically, although I let Craig believe that so he'd stay in the guest room. I didn't want him near me. I couldn't stand the sight of him—he looked so relieved, and so guilty about it.

I took a leave from my job at the gallery. I couldn't go in. I couldn't even get dressed. No one understood—to them the baby wasn't real. It was a medical event. But it was real, and it died. She died. Losing something you know is real that no one else even believes existed is lonely. Blood is certain though, if private.

Mr. Cosmo

After the wedding I was locked out of the bedroom. First it was to protect the sanctity of marital sex, I suppose, that tired old thing I'd seen before, and then for death and grief. A few days after the baby died—I knew it was gone because I'd known it was in there, I could hear its heartbeat and then I couldn't—Jack handed my leash to Phoebe and I stayed with her and Bill for a long time. It was peaceful there and I was happy.

Phoebe

She's taking it hard Jack said, when she told me about the miscarriage. She'd shown up on the porch one afternoon to ask if I'd be willing to watch Mr. Cosmo for a while.

I was happy to, despite the extra trouble. It wasn't just a favor, it was a pleasure. At night I'd lie in bed with Bill on one side of me and Cosmo on the other and listen as they twitched and chewed their paws and made little hiccupping sounds in their sleep. I felt grateful and surprised to be happy, sandwiched between them like that. I'd cup one of Bill's silky ears and feel his pulse beating inside it while he slept, and if it didn't help me sleep at least it calmed me down. In my other hand I'd hold Mr. Cosmo's stump. I'd watch the sheets rise and fall on us as we breathed together, feel Bill's bumpy spine lined up against my bare leg, watch the gelatinous rubble of my swollen body inside its extra-large flannel nightie as it rose and fell and think *it's come to this*. It wasn't what my life was supposed to have turned into but I'd learned to accept it and more, love it even. It was all I had.

That's the funny thing. Every day is its own universe, with its own portions of joy and sorrow. Maybe you can be happy anywhere. Surely you can be unhappy anywhere. I didn't even miss my other life, unless you consider fond remembrance missing, not even the ambitious sex that bed once had seen. I thought of the tremendous bulk it now supported, my two dogs and me, big as I am now. Together we must weigh over four hundred pounds, nearly twice the burden scrawny Duane and I were, back when I was svelte.

ROXANNE

For a long time I couldn't talk to anyone. No one understood. They all said it was for the best or if they didn't say it I could tell they thought it. My mother didn't even pretend to think otherwise and neither did Ruth, although at least she agreed it was sad and called every night for a while to pray with me. I stopped answering the phone though when she kept saying it was all part of God's plan. Phoebe, at least, didn't say a thing, just picked up Mr. Cosmo one night and kept him for two months. But I knew what she was thinking. People without children don't understand these things. Even Craig thought it was for the best. Especially Craig.

Oh, he was nice and helpful, he crept around the house and only vacuumed when I was in the shower. He kept April quiet and fed and dressed in clean clothes and I guess he did take care of me, brought me food on trays—scrambled eggs and toast, at first, cottage cheese, Jell-O, and then later on, when my appetite started to return, samples of his latest cooking experiments, a bit of artichoke and goat cheese pizza or shrimp fried rice—sometimes with a single spray of wildflowers in a bud vase on the tray. But I could tell how easy it was for him, that he liked me better as a patient than a wife. He almost enjoyed it, having me out of the way. I could tell he liked having the kitchen to himself, that his long face was just him making up for being relieved, not his feeling bad about the baby. He called her it instead of her. I had trouble forgiving him for that.

I told that to Gary, that I had trouble forgiving Craig. He'd started coming over when he heard what had happened. Ruth emailed him, told him to come. I knew failure to forgive was a sin, un-Christian, but somehow the longer I lay in bed the more it seemed like it was Craig's fault the baby was dead. Like she'd died from a lack of faith on his part, a lack of—let's face it—love. It seemed like if he'd wanted her, Patricia Jacklyn, more she would have felt it, would have wanted to survive and be born. Gary said no, it was God's will, that she'd gone to heaven to be with Him.

I didn't agree, but it didn't make me as mad when he said it. He'd started coming over to pray with me every afternoon and finally I had someone to talk to. At least he knew she had a soul. Gradually I started to feel better. I stopped praying for the pain to stop and started to pray for guidance.

At first nothing happened. It was the same feeling of staring into opaque water I always had when I prayed. I'd open my Bible to a random page the way Gary told me to and put my finger down, looking for the secret message intended only for me, and stare at my ragged fingernail pointing toward Nehemiah 11:29, *And at Endrimon, and at Zareah, and at Jarmuth,* and all I could think was how much I needed a manicure. It's not even a sentence.

I did it every day and I have to say that at the beginning it was discouraging. My faith was weak. But I kept it up. I lay in bed staring at the ceiling and praying for guidance and then one day I got it. One night I closed my eyes and opened my Bible and pointed my finger and when I opened my eyes I was looking at Matthew 19:14. *Suffer little children and forbid them not to come unto me for of such is the kingdom of heaven.* I felt a great warmth in my chest and fell asleep happy. I dreamt about Patricia Jacklyn. In the dream she was eating a pink cupcake. The next morning I woke up knowing what I had to do. What we had to do, I mean.

We were meant to adopt. I knew it. I knew the soul of that baby we lost was out there somewhere just waiting to come back and land in the body of April's little sister, even if Gary said that technically that wasn't the Christian view of things. I didn't argue—sometimes he seemed limited—because I knew I was right. After Gary agreed it was a good idea I talked it over with

Craig. As usual he didn't want to do it at first but then we all prayed together, Gary on one side of the bed and Craig on the other, each holding one of my hands, and when Craig realized it was God's plan for us he couldn't say no.

I started to feel better immediately. Gary arranged everything with a private agency. Gary was on the board; he wrote a letter of recommendation and got some of the fees waived. Being good Christians made up for some of our other problems and, in the interview, whenever they asked a hard question I was just honest. We were. We said we'd take it to the Lord in prayer. Gary even arranged for the church to help with the fees he couldn't get waived and that was a big help. If I ever had any doubts I kept them to myself. Doubt was just the devil talking. What were my puny doubts next to the joy of a baby?

Then they sent us the picture of May—she was Esmeralda back then—and that was it.

CRAIG

I know what you're wondering. Why didn't I leave then? Why didn't I get out when I could? After the baby died, after I'd dodged the bullet, after I'd done the right thing and been rewarded with a cosmic reprieve the gargantuan proportions of which I would never again in this lifetime see? What clearer sign of supernatural permission, guidance even, to get the hell out of town was there than that? Karen was all over me to. Why did I agree to the adoption?

Later, years later, Roxanne accused me of staying for the kitchen. It was a low blow, though maybe she was partly right. The truth is I didn't know where else to go.

ROXANNE

After my divorce from Drake I swore I'd never remarry. I meant it too. But something came over me when I met Craig, and don't laugh but I really thought this was it. Soul mates, true love and not just true love but true Christian love. I wanted to clean up my act, clean up my life. I wanted to consecrate our love.

"Ha," my mother said when I told her this. "Consecrate schmonsecrate. I know you."

The fact that my mother disapproved, not of Craig especially— they got along great—but of marriage in general, just made me want it more, to prove her wrong. My mother thought we should live together until eventually he left. That's exactly what she said—*until eventually he leaves*—and claimed not to understand why I didn't speak to her for weeks afterward.

"I just meant shack up why dontcha," she'd said, when I finally called her back. "Until the urge passes."

"I thought you liked him," I'd said.

"I do," she'd said. I could hear her scraping her teeth, picking tobacco out of her molars with the used toothpick she kept in her back pocket. "He's just not husband material. Men generally aren't."

When he first moved in she'd come for dinner almost every night—Craig invited her. He'd cook elaborate meals, although she and April would have been happy with hot dogs, and sometimes after I went to bed I'd hear them downstairs playing cards. He'd say he was going to clean the kitchen and come to bed later and then he wouldn't and I'd hear them at the kitchen table, gambling for quarters, him lighting her cigarettes, both of them laughing and her coughing, choking she was laughing so hard at whatever he'd said, until finally I had to go downstairs and tell them to be quiet, they were keeping April awake.

Of course I knew he didn't look like the best choice, but I couldn't stop myself. There was something about the way his hair curled away from his forehead after he took a shower, something about the way his jeans fit, or didn't, the way they were a little loose around the hips and slipped down, something about the way he looked with his shoulders back and his wrinkled blue shirt hanging open over a white T-shirt and jeans on a Sunday morning as he stood at the stove making waffles for April, flipping the broken pieces to Cosmo, low and slow so he could catch them. I had to have him. Who was it who said the heart wants what it wants? Someone who did something unspeakable, I think. But it's true. The more he tried to get away the more I had to have him. I can see now if I'd just let him go the way my mother said I should it would have all blown over and my life would be different now, better maybe. But the pain of those nights alone when he first left was too much.

The funny thing is, I never missed Drake that way. I suppose that's because I'm the one who ended it, finally. Maybe it was Craig always leaving or trying to that made me so crazy to keep him. I don't know. It's so easy to make up reasons afterward but really logic has no bearing on a thing when you're doing it.

All I know is that it felt good to want something that much for a change, even if it was doomed. Especially since it was doomed. With Drake it was all so programmed and appropriate. I never had a chance to want any of it. If it hadn't been for his parents we never would have married in the first place. I do remember liking his hair—April got hers from him, thank God—and liking the way he looked in his red swimming trunks from the back as he carried a cooler up the Michigan dunes on a certain August afternoon. The path was narrow and I walked behind him, carrying the beach bag, the blanket and the condoms.

Don't make me tell you every little thing about him—it's all so drearily familiar, embarrassing really. We knew each other in high school. He was fair. I was dark. He was smart and a jock. I was smart and an artist. His family had money. I, by comparison and within the narrow and excruciatingly calibrated class system of the suburbs, was poor. Our friends were friends. We were all nice and good looking and likely to succeed. The summer after college we met again, at his parents' club. I was waiting tables, before I started teaching. He was tending bar, before he started law school. We dated less than a year, then got engaged—Drake's father gave him money for the ring and plane tickets to Paris so he could propose in front of the Eiffel Tower. A month later we moved into an apartment in Lincoln Park and married a year after that. Now it all seems like staging, timing, romance. Was it also love? I can't remember.

The wedding took so long to plan that by the time it happened neither of us wanted it but by then it was too late to stop. His parents paid for everything, including my dress and the helmet-haired woman Elizabeth hired to organize it all. My mother wanted nothing to do with it, especially after I told her we weren't going with her idea of holding it at the VFW hall.

Elizabeth invited me to lunch one day to talk over the plans. She was still trying to like me then. "You're so creative," she'd said, "why don't you design the centerpieces?" She was smiling in that tight scary way of hers, trying to think of something she could trust me not to ruin. We were sitting in the members-only restaurant at the Art Institute—the one with white tablecloths I'd never been to—waiting for our asparagus quiche and Caesar salads and drinking big glasses of cold Pino Grigio when she'd said this. After lunch she steered me into the gift shop to buy thank you cards for wedding presents that wouldn't arrive for another six months. I wanted the Cy Twombly cards but she thought William Morris was more appropriate, for a bride. They were *so tasteful*, she said. OK I said. *Who cared*, I thought. She was paying.

Finally I did design centerpieces but she didn't like what I came up with and changed it all back to something *more classic* at the last minute. Not that I gave a rat's ass—it was just embarrassing, like everything else about the wedding. We had the reception at Drake's parents' club. Almost all the guests were from Drake's side. I was too embarrassed to invite any of my art school friends. It's all a blur now thanks to Valium though I do remember that I danced the rumba with one of Drake's uncles and later threw up pink grilled salmon and white chocolate cake with raspberry filling on the bathroom floor. The next day we flew to Athens for a twelve-day cruise.

WE STAYED in the apartment for five years, until we moved to the suburbs, and I wish we'd never left. I loved that old place with its cage elevator and bay window overlooking the park and big claw-foot tub in the bathroom. That apartment, that bathtub, and a black cat we named Eiffel, who died of fading kitten syndrome four months after we got her, are the only things about my first marriage I really miss.

The plan at first was that I'd support us while Drake went to law school. I liked the idea of being the breadwinner. Though I made so little—teaching art at a private elementary school— that Drake's parents said they'd help. After that the plan was to live on my salary while they paid Drake's tuition plus extras, but it turned out they paid for anything Drake wanted that we couldn't afford, which was pretty much everything. The apartment for sure, vacations, Drake's credit cards, our car. My salary ended up buying my clothes and our groceries, though we usually ate out.

I thought I'd like being an art teacher—I like kids, I like art—but I hated it. I hated that school. I hated trying to keep the attention of kids who saw me as one of their parents' employees. I hated being condescended to by ten-year-olds and hated the principal for letting them act that way. I hated the kids for bringing Thai stir-fry in their lunch boxes instead of peanut butter and jelly and for wearing shoes that cost more than I'd spent on my first car. I started to hate the way the faculty lunchroom smelled, like warm cheese and rotten lettuce and old tuna salad, and sometimes I even hated the other teachers, kind as they were in their big denim jumpers. I hated the way they were always so *upbeat*.

Roxanne, I was told in my review, *you need to be more positive. Children respond to teachers who are upbeat.* The other teachers were so *prepared*, always talking about their *goals* and their *lesson plans* and going to *conferences* to update their *skill sets.* Always coming in early and staying late to *decorate their rooms.* And not with anything the kids made in my class you can be damn sure but with gimmicky little holiday projects, hand-tracings of turkeys and leaf tracings and heart tracings, everything was a tracing, a copy of something else. When they ran out of things to trace they hung up big photo posters with inspirational sayings on them. *Hang in there,* they said, or *Believe in your dreams*—as if there's anything inspirational about photographs. Don't get me started on that. I still thought of myself as a painter in those days.

The kids wanted everything they did in my class to look like photos. *Art isn't about copying* I told them. *Art is about making.* I tried to teach them to invent, to be creative, though I thought it was strange. I shouldn't have to teach them that, should I? I thought it came naturally. Make something up I said, once even stamping my foot. But it was pointless, they didn't care about that and after the first few weeks, neither did I. It was more important to get them to clean up at the end of class, though I couldn't even get them to do that. They didn't know how. They all had housekeepers.

I felt bad. I knew I should be making my own work, and I tried to for a while, though it was hard to draw at night, after teaching all day. I'd set up a little studio in our apartment, in the sunroom off the living room, with a drawing table against one of the big windows. I'd started a series of soothing, to me, dot drawings in colored pencil on strips of torn dark blue paper that I'd faded in the sun so that the dark blue turned light gray at the bottom. Every night I'd sit at the window looking into the night sky drawing rows and rows of colored dots that became grayer and got smaller until they disappeared. They reminded me of night disappearing into dawn and working on them always put me to sleep. Disappearance was a soothing thought.

I thought if I ever got a show I'd hang the strips with push pins, just one clear pin at the top where the dots were brightest and densest and let them drop and curl at the bottom where the dots faded out. I thought of them as nightscapes and named them after constellations—Orion, Cerberus—someone's father had once pointed out to me on a Girl Scout camping trip. I was going to call the show *Sleep*.

I worked on the drawings while Drake studied or watched sports on TV. Baseball in summer and fall, then football, basketball, golf, all through the seasons, the pleasant drone and occasional roar in the background blending with the scratching sound of my pencils. I didn't mind. I preferred it to talking and it didn't interrupt my work, which was frankly mindless. Too mindless, I suppose—I never felt like a real artist. When I drew I didn't think about drawing at all or about any of the big ideas that had so excited me in college. I tried to, but they didn't interest me anymore.

It was a different kind of excitement I felt when I worked, the excitement of disappearing, that soothing numbness that was more like what I'd felt as a child when I hid under the porch with my coloring book and crayons. I felt safe, invisible. Sometimes I'd imagine having a baby, always a girl, the two of us coloring side by side in silence. Then Drake would shout and I'd look over and he'd pat the couch next to him and I'd happily abandon my drawing to watch some particularly thrilling play and pretty soon we'd have our clothes off, down in the couch, though he always kept one eye on the game. I didn't mind, I was relieved to be distracted. I still have those drawings, stored somewhere, rolled up in a cardboard tube.

As soon as my contract was up at the day school I quit and found the job at Lee's gallery. That's around the time I stopped drawing. The gallery job paid even less than teaching but what a relief—so quiet and nobody threw up on your shoes. Nobody threw paint. Nobody cried. Nobody squirted glue out the window or cut his neighbor's hair with blunt scissors when she wasn't looking. At the gallery I never had to yell *Quiet!* to make myself heard. The only time I ever raised my voice there was to ask *red or white?* at a noisy opening. If teaching had felt like missionary work, bringing faith to barbarians, working for Lee Hastings felt like a guaranteed lifetime junior membership in a very exclusive club.

Lee only showed abstraction. I liked that at first, it's why I applied there, and maybe it was my enthusiastic agreement with Lee's aesthetic that got me the job though it might also have been that his last girl had just quit to get married. I'd held up my left hand and wiggled my fingers, still proud of the enormous ring.

"You won't have that problem with me," I'd said, smiling.

"Then you're hired," he'd said, ignoring the ring and looking at my breasts.

Lee was dead serious about what he called his *no image policy*. When artists came in with work that looked remotely like something in the real world I was told to send them away and if they insisted on leaving slides—in those days everyone had slides—I was told to pitch them immediately. Under no circumstances was I to show the work to Lee. This was an important part of my job—protecting Lee from the visual insult of having to look at what he called *pictures of shit*. At first I thought this had to do with Lee's commitment to modernism, but after I'd been there a month, I heard him on the phone one morning.

I'm telling you. It's the only thing that sells these days. It's the new couch painting. Give 'em stripes that match the upholstery every time. He was twirling around in his yellow Eames swivel chair laughing, massaging his crotch as he spoke. *Market sucks though. Really? Really? Yeah. No. Me too. Two or three, that's it. No shit? Yeah. Yeah? Okay. You know what I say. If he can't drive it and she can't wear it they don't want it.* He looked up and saw me standing in the door with the mail. *Yup, hold on.* He waved me in. *Hey sweetie*—this to me, advancing politely with the *Wall*

Street Journal and what was left of the day's mail after I'd care-fully extracted and disposed of all offending artists' queries—*go get me another carrot juice would you?*

Sometimes, when artists slipped by, as Craig had, thinking they'd improve their chances by ignoring the girl, me, and going straight to the boss, Lee made them wish they hadn't.

Other things I did on my job besides throw away slides: sit at the front desk and answer the phone, sign for the work when it arrived, sign for it when it was shipped out, hand out catalogs to anyone who looked like a buyer and press releases to anyone who looked like press. Keep press or all but the very most important ones from mooching catalogs, which they were prone to do, unless they seemed like they seriously planned to write something. Call Lee if some walk-in said he wanted to buy something—rare but it happened. Help put up the shows, serve wine at the openings, clean up afterward, babysit the gallery while Lee schmoozed the collectors or disappeared for the after-noon. Buy birthday presents for Lee's kids and (soon to be ex) wife (size 8, favorite color black) and later, for his girlfriend (size 4, favorite color papaya). Manage the rental properties upstairs from the gallery, which Lee also owned and which, frankly, were his bread and butter, although no one was supposed to know that. I only knew because after a while I was the one who did the books.

"There's your real talent, sweetie," Lee had said to me once, after I'd showed him my work, hoping he'd give me a show. "You should have been an accountant."

And handle the artists. That was the only interesting part of my job. It's how I met Craig, though he claims not to remember. He'd brought in his piece for the summer group show that was being guest-curated by Nomi Yamakoshi, a friend of Lee's in town from Tokyo. She picked artists he never would have included and somehow Craig had gotten her attention and she'd invited him to put a drawing in and so there he was one day with his hair all askew and a rolled-up seven-foot drawing of a grubworm under his arm. The theme of the show was *Unseen, Obscene and Underneath It All*. It was Nomi's idea.

"Every piece must be provocative," she'd said at the meeting they let me sit in on. She'd frowned and punched the air with her tiny paint-stained index finger when she'd described to Lee what she had in mind, but except for Craig's giant grubworm, the show was kind of flat. Everything was either blandly abstract or predictably pornographic, with lots of delicate Prismacolor renderings of female genitalia and one large erect penis sculpted in pink-tinted beeswax, positioned atop a plaster Corinthian column from some architectural salvage place. When Craig brought his drawing in I'd thought *at least he's not doing that*. I thought it was refreshing and, frankly, cute that he was so out of sync. *A free spirit*, I'd thought as I helped him carry the big roll of Mylar back to the storeroom. But that was all. I was a married woman then.

So I worked at the gallery and made almost nothing. Lee didn't even give me health insurance. He expected that all his girls were either supported by their parents or well married, which, in fact, I was. By then Drake had joined a law firm and pretty soon he was making so much money it didn't make sense for me to work anymore, he said.

"Quit," he'd say whenever I complained about Lee. "We don't need the money. Let's get started on Project X."

Project X was the baby we planned to make. We'd agreed that after five years together it was time. All our friends— Drake's friends really—were either having them or talking about having them and Drake's parents were beginning to drop hints. So we tossed out my pills, bought a calendar and got to work. "Project X rhymes with sex," Drake said every time he marked the kitchen calendar with a red pen to schedule the coming month's optimal days for conception. For me it had a different meaning. X was the chromosomal team I was rooting for. I wanted a girl.

The day I brought the subject up with my mother was *an X-rated day*, as Drake called it, and we'd started early—at six or so—fast and efficient. I was still only half awake when Drake, all golden and pink, rose up out of the white sheets and said *time to make the doughnuts*. Five minutes later he'd given his finishing war whoop, flipped over in midair and dropped down beside me, panting. As I drifted back to sleep I felt him pat my belly. *That should do it*, he'd said, and got up to take his shower. I think he was right—I think that was the day April was conceived.

I had to deliver a painting to a collector in the suburbs that morning so, on a whim and a hunch, I called my mother and said I'd be in the neighborhood and asked if I could stop by for lunch.

"I want to tell you something."

I'd dared to say this to the back of my mother's head as she microwaved three pieces of leftover anchovy pizza. From where I sat at the cramped kitchen table, I could see how her spiky gray hair grew in a spiral around her little bald spot and stuck out on one side as if pointing to the nearest exit. She didn't reply, just stood with her stooped back to me until the timer went off and then shuffled over and set the paper plate with the pizza on it in the middle of the table alongside a roll of paper towels, two cans of Coke, a jar of peanuts and an overflowing ashtray.

"So shoot," she said.

My bare arms stuck to the vinyl tablecloth as I leaned forward to tell her. After I'd said the words—*trying pregnant baby maybe hope soon*—I picked up a piece of gummy microwave-ruined pizza and shoved it in my mouth. I took a too-big too-hot bite, just for something to do, trying to ignore the gritty little fish bones on my burnt tongue. I took another bite and another, eating without tasting, stuffing my mouth to keep it quiet as I waited for her to say something. Which she didn't at first. Instead, she looked everywhere but at me as she crossed her arms over her sunken chest, licked her teeth and tapped ashes onto the paper plate that held the remaining piece of pizza.

Finally she stubbed out the butt in the soggy cheese and said, "Well bar the door Katie. I guess now you'll see," and got up to clear the table.

I shouldn't have been surprised. "There but for the grace of God goes you," she'd said to me once in the grocery store when I was in high school, not even bothering to lower her voice as we'd passed some unhappy-looking young mother whose flushed whimpering toddler squirmed in the front of her grocery cart. I must have been fifteen. We were walking up and down the aisles looking for margarita mix. When I didn't respond she'd elbowed me for emphasis just as the child plucked a package of fig newtons out of the cart and dropped it on the floor with a loud splat. "There but for the grace of God," she'd repeated, satisfied to have made her point.

So her refusal now to be elated didn't come as a shock. Still, I was a little hurt. I'd been hoping for a cathartic mother-daughter moment. I thought she might be happy for me, or at least for herself. I think that's what I really wanted—to impress her with my ability to impress her, to cheer her up with that one certain thing, that perfect baby Drake and I were sure to produce. If that didn't work I was at a loss for what else to do.

I sat at the table biding my time and plotting my escape while I watched her run water into the sink. If I left too soon she'd taunt me for being thin-skinned. After what seemed like a safe interval, I stood up to leave. "Thanks for lunch," I said.

She turned from the sink and handed me the last piece of pizza, which she'd rinsed and wrapped in used foil. "Here," she said. "And about the other thing. Make sure you ask for an epidural as soon as you get to the hospital. If you wait too long they won't do it. You don't want that."

As soon as I closed the door behind me the cramped dark house disappeared. I felt the brightness and heat of the July day enfold me, burning off the shame of whatever had just happened. I climbed into my car, pushed the button to open the convertible top, gunned the engine and pulled away from the curb fast, free. It didn't matter what my mother thought. She had no idea how good my life was about to become. My real life, the one I was going to enjoy, was about to start.

We began house hunting in the suburbs. Drake's mother drove. We spent two months trooping in and out of other people's *lovely homes* as the realtor called them, smelling the apples baking in the self-cleaning ovens, put there to make the kitchens feel homey, admiring French doors and wraparound cedar decks, traipsing through sunny gabled nurseries, opening and closing enormous wood-veneered refrigerator doors and gazing into marble shower stalls as big as boxcars. The kitchens all had eighteen-inch high faucets. "For your pasta pots!" Elizabeth had said, fixing that pursed-lip Kabuki smile on me when she'd heard me wonder why. There were decorative Mexican tile backsplashes, heated slate floors, built-in temperature-controlled wine racks. I was awash in detail I hadn't known existed.

"Of course you'll want to sand the floors before you move in," the realtor said chummily, whisking me through a cavernous series of rooms she called the master closet suite.

"Of course," I agreed, eager to appear in the know. I couldn't have cared less until she said so, now I was already worrying about how wood dust would affect a baby I wasn't sure I'd conceived. Here I was back in the land where I'd grown up but *on the sunny side of the tracks* as my mother put it. Her dingy little ranch house was only three miles away.

"Let's start small," Drake had said, sensing how out of place I felt and putting his arm around me one Saturday afternoon as we stood on the front porch of a three-story, six-bedroom faux Victorian. To my relief, Elizabeth and the realtor agreed. After that it didn't take long for us to find *the perfect little house.* Actually Drake's mother found it, but I pretended I'd seen it first and that it was exactly what I wanted.

Elizabeth called it a honeymoon cottage though it had four bedrooms and most of the *gracious appointments* we'd seen in the other houses plus a few we hadn't, including a *luxury master bathroom suite* with gold faucets, a bidet and an enormous Jacuzzi in which Drake and I had sex—isn't that the idea?—exactly once and not successfully, and one of those enormous so-called gourmet kitchens with two of everything. "Parties, dear," Elizabeth had said with that perpetual clenched-jaw grimace of hers—was she grimacing at me or the idea of parties?—when I wondered why we needed two kitchen sinks. The pantry was equipped with what she and the realtor agreed was *a darling baking station.*

I waited to tell my mother about the house until it was too late to back out. Then I told her we'd bought a cottage. *Well whoop-de-do,* was her reply, when I told her where it was. A week later, on a morning I knew for sure that Elizabeth was volunteering at the hospital and wouldn't show up unannounced, I took her to see the place.

"I wouldn't call it a cottage," she'd said, panting as she leaned against the porch swing. She was exhausted from mounting the six steep front steps. When she'd caught her breath she added, "But I suppose you can always turn it into a funeral parlor if things don't work out."

"Wait until you see the kitchen," I'd said, breezing past her, ignoring the insult. I'd learned long ago the best way to combat my mother was to act oblivious.

I riffled through the welcome packet the realtor had left inside the door as my mother limped off to inspect the place. She disappeared into the kitchen and then reemerged shaking her head in the direction of the all-marble half bath. "How you going to keep this place up?" she said.

I looked over at her, standing in the middle of the big empty living room. Her back was turned toward me and she had her hands on her narrow hips, her thumbs hooked through the belt loops of beltless khakis that were sliding down her narrow hips, exposing the grayish top of her stretched-out underpants. Her bald spot looked bigger today and her oddly boyish shape reminded me of something my father had once said, at some boozy family gathering twenty years earlier. *That woman needs suspenders to hold up her girdle.* Everyone had laughed, even my mother. It mystified me as a child, but now I knew what he meant. Briefly I considered going to her and putting an arm around her bony shoulders. I didn't dare though—you never knew how she'd respond.

"Actually we hire cleaners, Mom," I said. "You know that." I knew it would irritate her, not only the fact of it but that she'd failed to make me mad. I couldn't resist adding, "And would you please not smoke in here."

"Yeah, yeah, yeah, I know," she said, flicking ashes in the direction of the fireplace. She didn't want to hear about it, not about not smoking and not about cleaners. She was miffed that Drake's parents had given us money for the down payment, miffed about the house being so big and new.

Everything happened at once. We found the house, I got pregnant, we moved, I quit my job. Now I was free to be an artist, at least until the baby came. I set up a studio in the bedroom next to the nursery and every morning after Drake left for work I went upstairs and sat at my drawing table for two hours before I started on the house. I tried to think of what I wanted to draw—constellations no longer came to mind now that my window overlooked the neighbors' air conditioning unit—but all I could think of was what I needed to do to get ready for the baby. I started drawing birth announcements—pink spirals—but then I stopped even doing that and when I got too big to sit behind the drawing table I got up one day and didn't go back. After that I kept the studio door closed. The sight of the drawing table made me feel guilty. Later we stuck a futon in there and called it the guest room though mostly we used it for storage. I never did finish the baby announcements. Elizabeth ended up buying engraved cards.

Five months to the day after we closed on the house April was born, difficult, perfect April, the spitting image of Drake, who never felt like mine. I loved her madly but she wouldn't nurse and within days of coming home she began to seem alien to me, a miracle of blondeness, more Drake's child than mine from the start. Or rather, Drake and Elizabeth's child—she looked nothing like me or either of my parents or even like Drake Senior. It was as if the rest of us had been skimmed, like muck, from the gene pool. Now Elizabeth, Drake and April were the essential family unit.

"This baby has good genes," Elizabeth had announced at the hospital, as she held April for the first time and gazed, relieved, down into the tiny pink face that was a smooth newborn version of her own old leathery one. I could see then how important it was to her, to all of them, that the baby looked like Drake, their golden handsome Drake, and not like me. I could see how until the baby arrived they'd all worried she might not. Even I was happy she favored Drake. Joy ensued all around, at least at first, until April and I went home and Elizabeth took over and I started to feel like a surrogate. If only the baby, April, were less beautiful, I sometimes thought as I watched her sleep, if only she looked more like me or my mother instead of like Elizabeth, with her long bones and yellow hair and cornflower blue eyes, I might have been able to love her more. Oh, not that I didn't love her. I did, I adored her. But she never felt like mine.

Drake and I fell apart after that. It took a couple of years but once it started there was no stopping the slide. Don't make me tell you what happened or why. I don't even know. Please don't ask for all the sordid details. It was the same old story or one of them at least. Take your pick. I fell in love with the baby and out of love with him. Or he fell in love with the baby and out of love with me. Or my becoming a mother made him confuse me with his mother and he stopped wanting sex. Or he fell in love with his work and out of love with me. Or his mother took over our life and squeezed all the love out. Or we never loved each other in the first place and he ran off with his assistant but then felt guilty and came back but it was never the same. Or I got bored being at home with the baby and went back to work and had an affair with a collector twice my age whose wife, he said, didn't understand him and had, he said, moved to their winter house in Boca Raton, except that she may have come back, calling out *I'm home!* outside their bedroom as if she hadn't really left him at all but maybe just gone to visit her sister for a long weekend and then come back early and found us drinking Sauternes and laughing about noble rot in their Victorian four-poster on their 800-count Egyptian cotton sheets at four in the afternoon. Just maybe that happened. And maybe that same woman, had this really happened, which I'm not saying it did, found my purse and took out my cell phone and pressed the home button and left a message for Drake, not that he would have cared at that point if any of this had happened, which I'm not saying it did, because he just might have still been screwing his assistant, which he claimed to have stopped, sometimes even in our Jacuzzi while I was at work. Or maybe when he found out his wife knew about us my lover shot himself. Or his wife shot him. Or she shot me, but missed. Or I left April with my mother and moved to a shack in the north woods and started painting again and took a succession of lovers from the local population of high school boys I hired to dig my well. Or Drake converted to Catholicism and became a Jesuit priest. All of the above, none of the above, some combination of the above, sort of. Take your pick. Obviously, I'm not comfortable discussing this. Does it really matter what happened or what I wish had happened? Who was it that said there are fifty ways to leave your lover? Whoever it was, was wrong. There are fifty million.

The fact is we broke up. The fact is things went seriously wrong in predictable ways and we thought we couldn't break up because there was a child and money and a house and in-laws and a special needs dog—by then we'd adopted Mr. Cosmo—but then despite all the complications we did break up and the truth is we should have done it sooner but we'd had this agenda that turned into April and then we couldn't end it but then we did and after that it was always a mess.

My mother said I shouldn't make such a big deal about it. She'd said this when Drake and I were in the midst of the worst of it, before we just gave up and ended it, when the therapist we were seeing said I should confide in someone. *Who?* I said and he suggested my mother, never having met her. This response— telling me not to make such a big deal of it—was exactly why I hadn't told her in the first place, but now it was too late.

"No point getting all het up about it," she'd said. "That's just how things work."

She was sitting in the porch swing with April on her lap when she said this, mashing up a banana with a spoon against the edge of a bowl as she explained the facts of life to me. According to her, biology made people have sex with people they normally couldn't stand to have lunch with so that opposite genes would mix together and the strongest ones would survive. As soon as a more or less perfect offspring was achieved the parties were free to go their own way and wise to do just that. "Hybrid vigor," she'd said. "It's how come we get such big vegetables now." According to her, if people only had sex with people they liked we'd all be a bunch of substandard idiots.

"Look at this kid," she'd said, indicating April who was waving her purple-socked feet up and down in rhythm as she gulped spoonfuls of banana trustingly from my mother. "Proof positive." My mother had revised her policy on babies as soon as she laid eyes on April, who, she was convinced, contrary to all evidence, looked just like her. Her new position on babies was that they were all a pain-in-the-ass except for April.

"Like it or not," she was saying, "it's the truth." She explained how nature kept couples together for exactly four years, long enough to get a baby born and raised to the point of walking and talking and peeing in a pot, and if you were dumb enough to have one at the end of the four years instead of at the beginning, well that was your tough luck. Time was still up. The attraction ended as sure as the music on the merry-go-round when the ride was over. Any fool knew when that happened it was time to get the hell off. One day you woke up and saw you were with the worst possible person you could be with and if you had any sense you moved on. Or he moved on, more like it.

"Biology," she concluded. "It frees the male to go spill his seed elsewhere. Anything else is just society trying to cram a pig's ear up a sow's ass."

"What?" I'd said.

She looked over at me as if she had no idea why I was upset.

"What about what?" she said.

I didn't know where to begin. "What about love?" I said, though I hadn't meant to. She had no answer for that except to make a sound in her throat reminiscent of the one Mr. Cosmo makes when he's getting ready to hork up grass.

It had been a rhetorical question. I knew my mother's position on love. It was like cat burglary as far as she was concerned. She didn't believe in it but if you had the itch the goal was to get in, grab what you could and get out without being caught.

I combed banana out of April's hair and we sat in discreet silence as the mailman approached. He limped up the path, dragged his bad leg up the front steps, scratched Mr. Cosmo behind the ear, smiled at April, dumped the mail into the French basket hanging by the door and limped back down to the sidewalk.

"If I'd done that, if I'd left Drake after four years," I resumed, when the mailman was safely out of earshot, "I wouldn't have had April." It was my only defense. Drake and I had been together almost seven years by the time she was born—if we'd done it my mother's way, April wouldn't exist.

I looked over to see her reaction. She had the baby perched on the lap of her beige polyester sweat pants, and was now feeding her torn-off bits from her own pink-frosted doughnut dipped in what remained of the mashed banana the way you'd feed a dog table scraps by hand.

"You know what I mean," she said, not looking at me and apparently unmoved by the suggestion that completely unnerved me, that any little flicker of fate, the wavering left turn of a single sperm, could have meant that our bright perfect star, April, would never have existed.

"No, I don't know what you mean," I said, angry now. "Explain it to me."

"Oh drop it," my mother said, unperturbed by her own faulty logic and bored with the argument now that she'd made her point. "All I mean is, it's not that big a deal. Let him go." She

70

tore off another hunk of doughnut and stuffed it into April's open mouth.

But breaking up was a big deal to me even though I was the one who wanted it. I felt embarrassed about failing and guilty about breaking up April's happy home. But I couldn't stand being married to Drake anymore, and I don't mean just the usual disappointments and irritations of marriage or even his family. I didn't really mind his family. I didn't even mind Elizabeth— looming over me all the time though she was, over six feet tall in her spectator pumps and wool suits and cashmere sweater sets for every season, fixing that beam of smiling disapproval on me. I was accustomed to disapproval, hers wasn't the first or the worst. I didn't mind Drake's sisters, both doctors—one a dermatologist, the other a urologist, one on either coast. I hardly ever saw them except when they came to the Midwest on alternating years for holidays, bearing expensive gifts for April. And I liked Drake's father, Drake Senior, Dr. Drake Reynolds, head of cardiology at St. Luke's Hospital, that silver-haired, red-faced, distracted man who, at a three-inch disadvantage to his wife, wore his hair puffed up to make himself look taller. He was nice to me though he rarely spoke. *The walking checkbook*, my mother called him. Everyone else in the family called him Senior.

I didn't mind the physical things that are said to cool a marriage either, the relaxing of the table manners, the finger in the mouth, the finger in the ear, the open bathroom door, the sight of the dirty drawers in the shared laundry basket, the other's toothpaste on the mirror, all that. Not that we ever shared a bathroom even in the apartment, which had two. Elizabeth advised us on that point at the outset, swore it was the secret to a long happy marriage, not that hers appeared to be happy. I never minded those things at all, even in the close quarters of the apartment. I liked them in fact. They kept me grounded in the physical world. Who was it that said the greatest poverty is not to live in the physical world? Whoever it was, was right.

It was something else I couldn't stand, not Drake exactly, but that uncomfortable feeling of knowing someone, or rather knowing they know you as well as they can and still knowing they don't know you at all. It was lonely, that so-called *intimacy*, the part that's supposed to be so *comfortable*, the pay off, the sweet soft center of melting together after you bite through the hard shell of getting to know someone. I preferred the hard shell. I don't mean I minded knowing him, I mean that I couldn't stand him knowing me, or knowing how little there was of me, rather, behind the surface attraction. Because honestly it didn't grow deeper, the way they say it does, it grew colder. Emptier, like walking down a long hall expecting to meet someone but then you don't. After a while I realized he had absolutely no idea who I was. It was lonely, like living in a de Chirico painting, those long shadows.

I told my therapist that. *My marriage is like a de Chirico painting*, I'd said, meaning it but also showing off, trying to see if he knew who de Chirico was. He'd cocked his head and nodded compassionately. That's one thing I did not repeat to my mother. She would have said that was just pure bullshit. *What were you expecting?* is what she would have meant.

Whatever it was, whatever went wrong, when the polish wore off and the fun wore off and the acting wore off and the house wore off and the thrill of eating mango sorbet naked at midnight straight out of the carton and then having sex on the kitchen floor in the glow of the open refrigerator wore off, we were just two polite strangers who loved the same child who didn't want to live together anymore.

The divorce was easier and cheaper than the wedding, faster too. Joint custody, no contest, April stayed with me. I kept Mr. Cosmo too. He was non-negotiable. I was prepared to fight for him, though it never came up, and I think the saddest moment of the divorce was when I realized Drake didn't even want him. That fact alone made me glad it was over.

I kept the house and most everything in it. If it hadn't been for April I would have moved and maybe I should have even so. But Drake insisted and his parents paid. I shouldn't complain. They smoothed everything over with money, lucky me.

I have to say, Drake's parents were never anything less than cordial when it came to divorce. Senior, on the rare occasions I saw him, acted like nothing had changed, and Elizabeth seemed to like me better for having ended it. Not that I really mattered to them one way or another except as April's keeper. What they cared about was her, access to April. We lived six miles apart—a bike ride away—and they wanted me there as long as they could manage it, ideally until she turned eighteen and was shipped off to the college of their choice. All it took was money, and they were *rolling in it* as my mother observed one day, looking out from behind the curtain as Senior backed his vintage Porsche convertible down the driveway, with one of April's pink flip-flopped feet sticking out the back.

So I stayed. Why not? I had nowhere else to go. Really it was amicable as these things go. April was so young, and Drake traveled so much, she hardly noticed the difference. All I wanted was out of the marriage and a place for April and me and Mr. Cosmo to live.

So I stayed in the house and went to the gallery three days a week—it didn't seem so bad anymore—and my mother watched April. I thought about going back to school, but I couldn't think of what to study. I was sick of art. That's when I went back to church and despite what my mother says, it helped a lot.

Not long after that is when I ran into Craig, fresh out of rehab. He seemed so fragile after Drake's imperviousness. I felt like I could have an effect on him. With Drake I never could. Craig was damp somehow, unfinished, like a newly-hatched bird, like a first grader with a stomachache on the first day of school. Drake and Lee and all the men I knew in those days, the collectors, even the artists, were all so fast and smooth, working so hard to get somewhere in life. They made me feel left behind, but Craig was going nowhere and I liked that. I suppose I mistook his problems for purity. Rehab—or maybe it was failure—had given him an aura of authenticity. Or maybe acting vulnerable was just how he got girls. It worked on me.

The first time she met him my mother called him a Huckleberry Finn. I don't know what that was supposed to mean—I doubt she'd read the book—but I thought of him as a diamond in the rough. His lack of ambition was disarming, refreshing, a relief. He reminded me of myself.

When he came into the gallery that day and asked to speak to Lee I remembered him right away from Nomi's show and when I said so he pretended he remembered me too. But I could tell he didn't, that he was just trying to charm me to get to Lee. I was a little insulted, not only that he didn't remember me but that he thought he could trick me into thinking he did. He said he was making *fundamentally abstract* work though I could see from his slides that he was lying about that too and I could see that Lee would hate it. Normally I would have done my job and explained that his work didn't fit our program and he would have left and that would have been that. But I let him through. Who knows why? I suppose I did it because by that time I was sick of Lee and his stupid mean ways and I knew Craig's work would infuriate him, and maybe also I did it to get back at Craig for not remembering me. At the time it seemed funny somehow, like a joke on both of them.

It might have ended with Lee throwing Craig out and neither one of them realizing I'd set the whole thing up. If I were a stronger person it would have ended there. But then, as he left, he gave me that impish look, the one I later came to hate but which at the time seemed so adorable, and the next thing I knew I'd dialed his number and left a message. When he called back he didn't even act surprised. He'd expected me to call, and that was another warning. I almost didn't go because of that. But I did, and when he told me he played in a Christian band something just clicked.

I'd been back at church for a year by then and everything looked different because of it. I'd shopped around. First, I went back to Redeemer Baptist, the church I'd gone to as a child, with Ruth's family, walking the block to their house every Sunday morning with a dime in my plastic purse to put in the offering tray. I went every week for seven years except for the year Sunday fell on Christmas, when I felt guilty leaving my mother home alone.

I quit when I got to high school. All that praying and singing seemed childish, but, later, in college, and after that, when I was with Drake, I missed it sometimes. I first noticed the feeling sitting in the dark in art history class in college, looking at pictures of Jesus on the cross. What I'd been taught in Sunday school was the only possible explanation for some of those paintings. I don't mean the doctrine—anyone can learn that—I mean the feeling, the ardor. I missed that.

I missed the comfort of sitting in those packed, sweaty pews surrounded by heavy adult smells—stale deodorant, face powder, menstrual blood, hair spray, and underneath it all another sourer smell, the metallic wool-scented aroma of masculine worry given off by the damp, wadded-up dollar bills that were fished out of men's suit pockets and dropped into the passing tray.

I missed the sound of all those voices raised together, singing those heavily accented, off-key hymns as Miss Darnell pounded out the dragging rhythms on the old upright piano in the corner. *Bless-ed re-deem-er, bless-ed re-deem-er, Hall-e-lu-jah, Je-sus is mi-i-ine.* She was always half a beat too slow. I was always afraid the song would grind to a halt before it was over, before we reached the long major chord at the end, like a car running out of gas. I missed it, though, that bound-together feeling I'd rarely felt since.

Though I had felt it, some kind of love I suppose you'd call it, a few times in the intervening years. I'd felt it once riding the el to work early in the morning, earlier than usual for a meeting and still sleepy but becoming aware that the edge of me had blurred into the edge of the dark meaty woman on the vinyl seat next to me as we rocked together on the vibrating train and I'd wondered if she even realized or cared that our molecules had blended in this astonishing way. Then she got off at Dearborn and it was over. I missed that anonymous joy I had regularly felt in church, the way all the out-of-tune voices came together to make up a perfect tuneless chord.

It was when April started talking and asking questions that I went back, but going back was harder than I'd expected. It felt strange after all those years, after everything that had happened. After my life with Drake, after all the money and the trips and the house and then April and the affairs and the divorce and therapy, it seemed odd to be back in the church of my childhood, like having lunch with an old lover. It reminded me of why I'd left.

The place was smaller and darker than I remembered, the construction shoddier and the rugs dirtier, the colors of the stained glass windows more garish. Without Ruthie and her six brothers and sisters sitting next to me in the hard pew, all of us pressed between the stern bookends of her parents, I was just an outsider. Everyone there who was my age was married. Even the solitary women looked married, looked like they were praying for the salvation of their wayward but at least still at-home-in-bed husbands. I was beyond all that. I was just alone, a fallen woman, and I couldn't get the old feeling back.

But I was determined to find at least a piece of what I'd lost. I tried other churches, eight to be exact, dragging April along with me, until eventually I found Willowbrook. It hadn't been my plan to go to such a big, synthetic place but I came to like it. It was new and clean, all hope and no history, with something for everyone. It was big enough that April and I could keep to ourselves. At the smaller churches we stood out. Everyone wanted to hear our story and I didn't want to tell it. At Willowbrook we were anonymous and we came to feel at home.

Craig was the first religious person I met on my own after that, away from church. It felt significant, like he was the link that connected my two different lives into one. Meeting him made me feel like I'd finally moved on. It seemed like proof that I'd changed, that I was attracting better people. The fact that he was in rehab didn't scare me at all and when he told me about Golgotha it seemed like a sign.

So I invited him to church. It was an impulse but it felt right and that whole week, after I'd asked him and before we went, I felt better and better. After the service I introduced him to Gary and he told Gary about the band. Gary said he'd tell Ron, the minister of music, to give him a call so they could talk about a gig. It all just seemed to be falling into place. Later Craig claimed I'd tricked him, that I'd pretended there was a gig just to make him come back, but that's ridiculous. He's the one who didn't follow up. Then after a few weeks I invited him to my fellowship group.

I wasn't sure it was a good idea. I talked it over with them before I brought him—that was the rule since it was supposed to be singles only, no couples. I said he was just a friend and they said in that case it was all right. The next week Craig came with me to the meeting and we all prayed for guidance and afterward they told us they didn't think it was appropriate for us to start dating, if that's what we had in mind, since my divorce was so recent, and I told them we weren't dating, we were just friends. Craig looked at me and nodded. Besides, I thought, Craig and I had our celibacy vows in common.

Everyone in my fellowship group—Second Time Singles— had taken a vow of celibacy until remarriage. It was a condition of joining. You could bring guests a few times but if they wanted to join, they had to make the pledge. Otherwise, Pastor said, it was like inviting a wolf into the chicken coop.

It wasn't a casual thing. There was a twelve week course of counseling and then, if you and your pastor agreed you were ready, a candlelit ceremony at dawn on a Sunday morning. We all wore long white robes and the women accepted a Second Time Virginity ring from the pastor. The men got a lapel pin in the shape of a cross, though I never saw any of them wear it. Most of us were divorced women.

I knew what my secular friends would think of all this, especially art people. Married to Jesus and all that. I didn't tell any of them or anyone else. Not Phoebe. She wouldn't have understood. I didn't even tell Ruth. And I certainly didn't tell my mother, who'd let it be known she thought religion was all a crock when I first started going to church when I was eight. Once a year she came to see me in the Christmas pageant and sat in the back, smirking, trying, but not very hard, not to laugh as she stared into her upside down hymnal. She didn't even pretend not to be glad when I stopped going. So I didn't tell anyone about my vow except for Craig.

I see now that it was a mistake to bring him to my fellowship group. Some of the more fanatical members challenged our commitment to celibacy. Donny, my peer counselor, said she thought Craig had a worldly air about him. Then one night after a meeting they called us aside, separately, to talk to us and after that Craig wouldn't say what happened but said he didn't feel welcome anymore and quit. So I stopped going too. We got together not long after that so we would have had to drop out anyway. People can be so mean. We didn't invite any of them to the wedding.

Early on it was good, I swear it was. Everyone says look to the beginning, the fault lines were already there, and I suppose so now—well, obviously they were—but that's just one way to look at it. Anyone can predict failure. Everything fails eventually. Believing that it won't, that's faith. All I mean is that there was a little while, before I got pregnant, when it was good, great even. Even if it was just for a few days, or a few minutes, the taste of it gave me something to believe in.

Craig would hang around the house while I was at work. He'd vacuum and sometimes he'd cook dinner and sometimes the guys, boys really, from Golgotha would come over to rehearse and hang out.

They'd be there when I got home from work, walking around in their stocking feet—Craig made them take off their shoes—wearing flannel shirts over their T-shirts and jeans. Or I'd find them sitting on the couch—all of them in a row—in front of that huge TV in that big fancy living room where I used to have to serve drinks to Drake's parents, and they'd be watching cartoons or some ball game and April would be sitting barefoot and cross-legged on the floor in the middle of it all, with her big box of crayons, coloring at the coffee table, and I'd think *There. Now this is a family.*

April loved it, loved them. And why not? They were nice guys. In those days they didn't even drink. They all drank soda, that's what they called it, *soda*, like children. I bought it for them by the case. It didn't even matter what flavor, just that it was fizzy and sweet. And they were so polite—*May I have another soda please? Thank you.* Then Craig would come out of the kitchen wearing oven mitts, carrying a casserole, or a pizza he'd made himself, and we'd eat dinner off the coffee table and they'd all sit around and play music and tickle April and make up these games. One time Tim yelled *Hey best cover version ever—don't think about it just say the first thing you think of.* And Todd said *Gotta be Blinded by the Light, Manfred Mann, 1977*, and Spence yelled *No way* and flung a slice of pepperoni at Todd, a greasy miniature Frisbee, and Todd reached up and caught it in his fist like a fly ball. So graceful! It made a little splat sound when it hit his hand. At first no one said a word, we were all so surprised, and then Craig said *Out!* like an umpire, and everyone laughed.

I was standing next to Craig who was sitting on the couch and he'd put his arm around my hips and everyone was laughing and he'd slipped his hand down inside the back of my skirt inside my underwear without anyone seeing and that day at that moment I was as happy as I've ever been. I loved them, the boys, and I loved Craig the best. It was like I was one of them but also like they were my children. It was perfect, those weeks. Or at least I thought so. I had no idea.

CRAIG

I like to cook. I always did. Even as a kid I liked to experiment in the kitchen. I remember sitting in ninth period algebra class, freshman year in high school, planning what I was going to make for my lunch the next day, thinking about how Thousand Island dressing would taste with tuna salad and iceberg lettuce, on white bread with butter—or would it be better on toast and would the toast stay crisp until midday?—and that would get me thinking about how it would taste on grilled cheese on rye with sweet pickles and tomatoes. Making my own lunch was the only time I got to use my mother's kitchen and having my own kitchen was my favorite thing about college.

I like to cook for women. And they like to be cooked for, sometimes too much. Roxanne was like that at first. She always thought it was *so seductive,* such *a metaphor.* She'd lick her lips when she said this like I was going to drop everything and throw her on the floor right then and there. *One thing at a time* I'd have to say when she'd start brushing up against me when I was trying to concentrate on boning a fish. I had to tell her some-times food really is food, not foreplay.

Although. I do like to watch a woman eat. I like to see a girl gorge herself when she thinks no one's looking. When I was a student, at the School of the Art Institute, I'd walk though Grant Park on my way to class, back when it was just bums on benches with pee on their pants and newspapers over their faces, before they turned it into a circus for tourists, and I'd see all these working girls eating their lunches out of bags, just stuffing food into their mouths so fast they left crumbs on their faces. It was exciting to me. They looked so hungry. I love seeing a girl give herself pleasure that way. Pleasure is private but eating is public.

It's more than interesting. It's something you can watch a girl do without anyone thinking you're a perv.

I used to like to walk around my old neighborhood in Wicker Park just as it was getting dark and watch the girls in the diners and sandwich shops eat their dinners. I'd see them sitting alone by the windows, their eyes hooded and mouths open, with forks and wet fingers going in and out, between their greasy lips. I'd walk past and turn around and walk past again. Then I'd go home and draw them. I know what you thought I was going to say. I'd do that, too. But then I drew them, to remember.

I always noticed what they were eating. Salads usually, or burgers. Sometimes just a big plate of French fries. I remember one girl, woman, whatever, she wasn't that young, in a booth at Bea's Diner, with a *Chicago Reader* spread out on the table in front of her and dark hair falling across her face. She was wearing glasses and eating an omelet, with toast. It was dusk, about seven-thirty, eight o'clock at night and it got to me, an omelet at that time of day, maybe because that's my specialty. I thought to myself, *I want to make that girl an omelet.* I wanted to make her the omelet of her life. I thought about it a lot, what I'd put in it. Maybe just goat's cheese and bean sprouts, I thought sometimes, with a few chives, something minimalist and elegant. Other times I'd imagine something extravagant, loaded with tiny shrimp and crabmeat, red onions, Brie, mushrooms and capers, with pesto toast on the side. I went back every night after that, for weeks, but I never saw her again. I promised myself if I did I'd go in and talk to her but it never happened. It's just as well. Val would have killed me. I got a lot of drawings out of it though.

It isn't just women I like to watch eat. I watch everyone. Watching someone eat is a way to get to know them in a way you otherwise never would. Though it's usually sad, all that desire, especially when someone eats alone. It's embarrassing sometimes. Some old guy with white stubble on his chin and his hair sticking up, the kind of guy you'd look away from on the street, stuffing a burger into his open mouth. Sad. Almost obscene. You know what he'd look like jerking off. Sometimes walking up Milwaukee Avenue I'd pass one of the grimier burrito shops and see some guy, all alone, eating a big sloppy plate of Mexican food under a fluorescent light, just staring into space, chewing, a shiny grease mark across his chin and there would be that blank pleasure look on his face and I'd just want to cry. Or not want to, I would. I'm very careful about eating in public. I stay away from windows.

Roxanne

When I got back from Lima with May everything was a mess. Craig and I were on the verge of divorce. Our finances were a disaster. The basement had flooded. The mailman wouldn't deliver our mail because there was a beehive on the front porch. And we had an oddly unresponsive baby on our hands with only one grandparent to help this time instead of the three I'd had with April. Craig's parents eventually warmed up to the idea of a brown grandchild but they lived two thousand miles away.

At least my mother didn't care about May's skin color. But it took her a while to get over the idea of adoption. *So you're gonna buy one this time?* was her reaction when I'd told her the plan.

Things got better after she stopped referring to May as a *ringer*.

"Mother," I'd said, so angry after I'd looked the word up that I thought I would strangle her, "she is not a ringer. She is my daughter, and until I disown you, she is your granddaughter."

"Yeah yeah yeah," she'd said, jiggling May in midair and whispering *you little ringer* in her ear. But she'd managed to coax a small smile from her, which was more than I could do.

The first thing we had to figure out was child care so I could go back to work full-time. Luckily, Lee needed someone to manage his rental properties and we patched things up on the condition that he give me health insurance and a raise. The plan was for Craig to be a stay-at-home dad. "Can't you call it something else?" he'd said, pulling on his hair. "I hate that expression." But I didn't see why.

At first I'd pushed him to get a real job, but when I saw the kinds of jobs he was applying for I changed my mind. "You want to be an artist," I said, "go for it." Later he told the therapist he felt I was making fun of him, that I was punishing him by trapping him at home with a baby. But I'd meant it. Why couldn't he combine fatherhood with making art? It wasn't like he was totally housebound. My mother was more than happy to cover for him when he taught his one class per semester at the community college. He got plenty of social life doing that, all the fawning nineteen-year-old girls in tight jeans he could handle. And Golgotha still got an occasional gig. I thought he could spend his days making art and watching May and April and that once he got a body of work together he'd find a gallery and start to sell. I always thought his work was good.

"I can't work and watch a baby, Roxanne," he'd said. "Even if I wanted to. I don't know the first thing about babies."

I suppose he was right. But even when my mother started coming every day to watch May it wasn't like he was painting any more than he had been or that his work generated any income. If anything, it cost us. But whenever I asked him about money all he'd say was that he was *working on it.*

It seemed like he spent more time in the kitchen than he did in his studio. One day I found his recipes. "This could pay off big time," he'd said, looking embarrassed, when I asked him about the three-ring binder filled with ingredient lists and dated contest entries I'd found stashed on a back shelf in the pantry when I was looking for matches.

After that he didn't hide it. He'd sit at the kitchen table with my mother, leafing through women's magazines, tearing out pages and putting them in piles, one for pictures he was going to use in his collages, another for recipes and a third for contest entry forms. He was always experimenting. "Taste this," he'd say, handing me a forkful of piecrust he'd made from crushed gingersnaps, lemon juice and butter. "Do you think it's too snappy? I could tone it down with graham crackers." He planned to fill the crust with banana pudding and enter the recipe in the You-Need-a-Chiquita-Banana contest.

Or he'd say, "This one is going to change my life"—he never said our life—and head off to the post office on his bicycle with his Bays English muffin pizza recipe in the back pocket of his jeans. When I asked him why he was gone so long he'd say he was at the library, researching the history of garlic.

He entered every contest he could find—Mad about Mushrooms, Mrs. Butterworth's Pancake Flip-Off, Oh Boy Oatmeal, Pot Pie Pourri. Once he even won a case of molasses for an honorable mention in the Molasses Surpasses contest for his chili recipe. They were all just a rehearsal for the big one, he said. The Pillsbury Bake-Off. That was the one he was always talking about and planning for. Grand prize was a million dollars.

"A million dollars, Roxanne. Imagine." He was kneading creamed corn and dill into bread dough at the kitchen counter, explaining why he wasn't going to apply for the assistant sales job I'd told him about. "That's twenty years of some crappy salesman salary."

"Not that crappy," I said.

"A million dollars isn't that much after taxes." This observation came from April, who was at the kitchen table, doing her homework. She must have picked it up from Drake. Sometimes she scared me.

"Don't you worry, sugar pie," Craig had said, flipping the dough in the air and catching it behind his back. "That's only the beginning."

He had a theory that sweetness was passé. Everybody was sugared out, he said. He thought the next winning recipe would be some kind of bread using herbs, dill probably, fennel maybe, and he was baking a new herb bread once a week until he came up with a winner. He kept little pots of sage and basil on the kitchen windowsill and in the summer he put them outside and got April to help him water them.

In some ways, eventually, after things settled down, after I got used to the idea that Craig and I weren't the love match I'd thought we were, it was a nice life, despite the fact that we slept in separate rooms. Something good was always in the oven, and Craig was good with the girls, especially as May got a little older. We were a family, if not a particularly happy one.

My mother had fallen in love with May and ended up doing most of what Craig called the babysitting, which I had to keep pointing out to him wasn't babysitting when it's your own child. Phoebe offered to pitch in too. She said I could bring May over with Cosmo any time I wanted and that she'd watch them both. It was sweet of her but I had no intention of doing that. I wasn't sure if she understood the difference between a baby and a dog. What if something happened, what if there was some disaster, a fire or a flood or something, and she had to leave the house? I didn't trust her to know what to do.

But all that came later. Child care turned out to be the least of our problems. The main thing we had to figure out when I got back with May was us. We were a wreck.

I'd cried the whole way back on the plane just thinking of how I didn't want to go home to Craig. I felt sorry for myself, of course, but even sorrier for little May. Her life had already been so hard and despite my best intentions I was bringing her back to a home filled with strife.

I entertained some desperate thoughts on that flight. I thought about running away. I even wished the plane would crash, that we'd be the only survivors, in some jungle, and that no one would know where we were. I wished the plane would be hijacked and that we'd be forced to live the rest of our lives somewhere else. Anywhere else. I didn't want to go home and I'm ashamed to admit it but I wasn't even thinking of April.

All I could think was that I didn't want to see Craig. But then when he wasn't there at the airport I realized I had wanted to see him at least to tell him what I thought of him and then I got home and he still wasn't there and by the time he showed up at the house I wanted to kill him. If we hadn't had May to think about we would have just ended it then, that day.

But it was too late for that. Wasn't it? Didn't little May need a father, after all she'd been through? A daddy's shoulders to ride on? Or that's what I thought at the time.

So we went back to counseling. Right away, the next day. We had to. When he walked in the door that afternoon carrying April, I said *I don't know what I'm going to do, maybe I'll just kill you, maybe I'll just suffocate you right now with this dirty diaper* and he covered April's ears and said *don't do this Roxanne* and I said *no I mean it* and he said *I know you do* and then he'd suggested—he suggested!—that we call Pastor Gary. I said are you kidding? And he said no and I said I can't talk to Gary about this and he said maybe we should find someone else.

We'd been in therapy before—a lot of good that did—but Craig didn't like the therapist so we quit. We'd gone for two months, when I'd found out about Karen the first time, the first time I was supposed to go pick up the baby. Craig was going to stay home with April while I was in Peru and he'd dropped me off at the airport and then left to pick up April at school and drop her off at Elizabeth's for a few hours, but my plane was late and then I got a message from the adoption lawyer saying the hearing was delayed and that I should go home and wait, that it might be days or weeks. So I called Craig to pick me up but he didn't answer so I called my mother. When I got home Craig wasn't there and when I called his cell it was still off. So I looked around and the idiot, the complacent idiot, had taken a phone message from Karen and written it down and circled it. With a heart. That's how I found out. After that it was easy—I looked her up on caller ID.

I have to tell you, it was a shock. I mean literally, like an electrical shock. All of a sudden everything that hadn't made sense fell into place and I got in my car and drove to her house and there was my car—my car!—parked in her driveway. Thank God I didn't go in. I'd planned to but I didn't. I just drove home and waited and when he came home I told him I knew everything. Although it turned out I didn't, yet. I found out on the first night of therapy that the affair with Karen hadn't just started. I found out then that Craig had been seeing her the whole time we were together. Even before we got married. He'd met her at church, in my singles fellowship group.

I found this part out while sitting in a red vinyl chair in the office of Rick Morris, or Dr. Ricky as he told us to call him or Dr. Rigor Mortis as Phoebe called him when I told her about it, years later, about how he just sat there and listened to us fight.

"Wait," I'd said, when he said he'd been seeing Karen the whole time. I thought I was having a stroke. The lights were dimming. I was dizzy. Maybe I was going to throw up.

"What?" I said. Tunnel vision. Roaring in ears.

"Please sit down, Roxanne," said Dr. Ricky, looking worried. He'd seated us in matching easy chairs on either side of a small round table that held a clock and a box of tissues.

"Roxanne, come on." Craig was talking now. "We were just friends then, you and me. Remember?" He smiled horribly, showing lots of teeth. "You told everybody we were just friends. That's what we agreed, remember?"

He was smiling the way terrified people smile, maybe hoping if he smiled I wouldn't kill him. "What?" I kept saying. I was thinking about how we'd talked about inviting Karen to the wedding. Craig had said no, and I'd said I thought you liked her and he'd said sort of, but isn't she kind of weird? And I'd said well, sort of. And then we'd laughed.

"Wait, I don't understand," I said again.

"It's complicated, Roxanne."

"Complicated?"

"Sit down, Roxanne."

"No. Wait. Do you mean that night you went home instead of staying over, when you said you couldn't stay because you had to get up early the next day. That night?"

He nodded, still smiling that horrible death's-head smile.

"It started that night," I said.

He shook his head no.

"Wait."

"Before."

"Before what?"

"Before us."

"What?"

"Come on kids, I don't think this is productive," said Dr. Ricky, who was someone we'd found in the phone book. He looked nervous.

We both ignored him.

"Before?"

He nodded, still smiling.

"What about your vow? Your big fucking celibacy vow?"

"That was real," Craig said, his voice suddenly deep and serious. "I really did do that." He seemed relieved, proud we'd finally hit on something he'd told the truth about.

"You broke it, your vow, for her?"

It was too much.

"Sit down, Roxanne," Ricky said, louder this time.

"I'm sorry, Roxanne," Craig said, looking afraid.

"Sorry? You're sorry? Sorry you did it or sorry you got caught? Or sorry that now and for the rest of my life I'm going to be biding my time until I can figure out the best way to kill you?"

"Roxanne, sit down."

"I'm just sorry, OK?" Craig said. "I'm sorry for everything. Sorry I was born." He added this last flourish quietly, in a new self-pitying tone that sounded practiced. It occurred to me it wasn't the first time he'd said it. He'd said this to other women, I realized, maybe even to Karen. He knew how to keep apologizing until people got sick of hearing it. The boredom of it calmed them.

Dr. Ricky clapped his hands together, wrote me a prescription for Valium and made an appointment for the following week.

It was never the same after that. It didn't just change the future; it changed the past. What I thought the past had been, it hadn't. Even though the part I'd thought was so great had only lasted a couple of months, less than that, a few weeks really, I thought we'd had a perfect moment. But I guess not.

At first I didn't tell anyone. Then I told Ruth and she said she'd always had a bad feeling about Craig. She said she'd pray for us, but the way she said it made me realize she was pleased to be right. Phoebe didn't seem surprised either, but at least she didn't say so. I didn't tell my mother. I knew she wouldn't be surprised. I knew what she'd say, which is what she did say when she finally did find out. *Here we go again.*

She'd have said, and later did say, if I hadn't been so pushy it wouldn't have happened at all, or at least wouldn't have gone so far and so far off track. It could have just been a fling, she'd say. Or not even that, a passing crush that would have been over in a month. She would have said and then did say that in her opinion I knew all along what was going on and pretended not to so I could blame Craig for the whole thing when really he was trying to tell me so I would do him the favor of ending it. She'd have told me, and then she did tell me, to kick him out, or not even that, to just let him go, and to let him take his favorite frying pan with him, the fancy one I got as a wedding present the first time, because I was never going to use it. I could just hear her say all this and then she did.

"He's not a bad guy," she said, "but he's not the kind that sticks around. Ease up why don't you." *Why dontcha.*

Actually she'd said that the first time she met him—he'd roasted a lemon chicken for the occasion—and afterward she'd said, "Cute guy and he sure can cook. But don't expect that one to stick around."

I argued back, in my head, that I was glad the whole thing had happened with Craig, even though it had turned out badly. I was glad because I got May out of it. What I didn't say even in my imaginary argument was that I wasn't even glad the way I was glad about getting April from Drake. I was even more glad. I had to share April. But May, May was mine in a way April could never be.

But I didn't want to have that argument with my mother and as it turned out I didn't have to. Craig's the one who ended up telling her, at least his version of it, one night during one of their card games after I'd gone to bed. I heard them down there late one night laughing, playing hearts or poker or whatever it was. Gradually they quieted down except for a low mumble and the slap of cards on the kitchen table and the occasional fake curse from her as she let him win. The next day she told me he'd told her all about his girlfriend *so you can stop faking it now about your happy marriage.*

That hurt. He'd gotten to her first, charmed her. "I'm not faking it," I'd said. "I'm just trying to make it work, unlike some people." I never asked either one for the details, what he told her. I knew whatever it was he'd managed to make it my fault, managed to make himself sound sympathetic.

It was just one more thing to forgive. It was exhausting. There was already so much and I couldn't seem to get started.

CRAIG

Money was the real problem. Roxanne expected me to get a job, a regular nine-to-fiver. One minute I'm this guy, an artist, perfectly happy or maybe not happy but OK and recovering and celibate and living in three shitty but at least my own rooms in Wicker Park and dealing a little dope on the side but not using and the next minute I have a wife and a girlfriend and a mother-in-law and two kids and a house in the suburbs and I'm going to church and cleaning the gutters for God's sake and looking for a job.

What kind of a job did she expect me to get? I was an artist. All I'd ever done was wait tables and work the cash register at Pearl Art along with all the other green-haired, eyebrow-pierced, tongue-studded art students. Nothing against them, but I'd aged out of it. Been there done that, for five years. That's where I met Val, my first and only tongue stud.

"What do you want me to do, go back to waiting tables?" I'd said. I thought the answer was obvious, but Roxanne gave me that big old pitiful hopeful grateful Roxanne look and I realized she thought I was serious.

"Would you be willing to?" she'd said. *Over my dead body*, I'd thought, though I didn't say it.

I did work some. There was the adjunct teaching thing—I loved my students, but we all know what that pays—and there were the occasional Golgotha gigs though those weren't much better. It never turned into a regular thing with the church, probably because Gary and I couldn't stand each other. Or maybe because of the mix up about money.

When I brought it up, after we played the first time and a month had passed and we still hadn't been paid, he acted surprised and said he hadn't realized the band expected to be paid. He thought we meant it as an offering, he said, *a way to give back.* He'd slapped me on the back when he said this, looking all smarmy and hurt at the same time. Then I had to say sorry but no that's actually not what the guys had in mind. But I thought *Offering my ass, you cheapskate. As soon as I get something, I'll think about giving some of it back, but first things first.* It was embarrassing though. As usual I was the one who was made to look like a jerk.

Somehow I had to bring some money in. It was one thing living in a shit box studio apartment with the occasional handout from my mother or my grandmother, but supporting Roxanne and May in the suburbs was something else. Not that I was supporting them exactly but even the little things added up. Gas, art supplies, groceries. My life had become a nightmare, all because of one errant sperm that didn't even become a person. Now I was expected to be responsible for all these people, and I felt like I was always letting them down. Karen says my problem is that I'm too compassionate, or she used to. Now she has a new boyfriend and isn't speaking to me.

At least Roxanne got the house, thanks to Drake, or, rather, thanks to his parents. Drake's a good guy, by the way, kind of white bread but very nice. I'd see him when he'd come to pick up April and he was always polite. We'd talk about sports. *How about those Cubs,* he'd say. I never told him I'm a White Sox fan. *How about those Bulls? How about those Bears?* I had no problem with him. I liked him, when I wasn't envying him, the cool way he could just pick up April and leave, leave me there in his ex-house with his ex-wife and his ex-dog while he just drove off in his big-ass Range Rover all freshly vacuumed and clean. It didn't matter to him if April dropped Cheerios on the floor or if Cosmo went along and drooled on the dashboard and leaked urine in the back seat. Some guy working for minimum wage at the car wash would just vacuum it out and polish it up for him and even if he did a half-assed job Drake would still give him a nice tip. The only one vacuuming my car was me. I admit I envied those crisp clean shirts of his, always tucked in, even on a Saturday morning. His fingernails were always filed. You wouldn't think I'd notice things like that but I do. He had perfect cuticles. And those teeth. Even his jeans were perfect, with creases ironed into them. I wondered if he had them dry-cleaned. I don't think he had any idea how different his life was from mine, how easy it was, compared to mine. Not that he ever would have thought about it. That's the point. He wouldn't have. Why would he? Now there's a guy with something to give back.

Frankly, I couldn't figure out why Roxanne left. I once heard her talking to Phoebe about him. *Implacable*, Phoebe had said, shaking her head. I looked it up. It means unstoppable. What's so bad about that?

Roxanne wasn't doing so bad herself, though you couldn't convince her of that. Drake's parents owned the house, but Roxanne lived there for free. I mean we did. She complained they made it impossible for her to move, but that wasn't really true, and besides, why would she want to? They supplied everything April could ever want—a baby grand piano was delivered on her seventh birthday. I called Drake's parents the ATF squad—April Totally Forever—until Roxanne told me to shut up. Nothing wrong with that, though, if you've got the money.

At first Drake's parents weren't too happy about me showing up in April's life. That was obvious. They even hired a lawyer to do a background check to make sure I wasn't some kind of criminal and I was worried for a while, but the drug stuff never came up. Later Roxanne told me they were checking to make sure I wasn't a registered sex offender.

"You gotta register for that nowadays?" Jack had said, making light of the whole thing when I told her about it. At least she was on my side. After Drake's parents satisfied themselves I wasn't some child molester, they got used to me. I wore them down. I'd always send April to their house with something good to eat. I think the Concord grape pie finally did it. After that, Elizabeth began to ask me for recipes.

"You should be happy, Roxanne," I said, when she'd start to complain. "You got no worries. Look at me." I'd said this during one of our fights about money. We had a pre-nup and separate bank accounts, and she thought I was hiding money from a trust from my grandmother, which, honestly, I had been, but by then it was gone. We fought about who was worse off. She yelled back, "I've got no worries, you asshole? I'm looking at my worries."

She'd meant me. Then I turned my back on her for a minute—not to walk away, I swear, just to check on the custard-filled corn bread I had in the oven to make sure it wasn't getting too crisp around the edges—and she slammed me in the back of the head with one of April's American Girl dolls. I think it was Kirsten. She swung it by the ankles and I could see one of its little patent leather shoes fly off and skid under the refrigerator just as the hard plastic connected with my ear. One thing I learned early on about Roxanne—never turn your back on her in a fight.

But back to the house thing. Drake's parents had that much money. Roxanne really blew it there. She should have done everything she could to keep that guy around. At least April was all set—clothes, toys, music lessons, vacations. They took her to Spain when she was eight to see the Goyas at the Prado. I still haven't been. They promised her college wherever she wanted, and anything she wanted they gave her. Harp lessons, riding lessons, ballet lessons, a full-sized trampoline, and not one but two oil portraits, one for their house posing in a black velvet dress next to their Scottish terriers, the other for us, in pink satin, with Mr. Cosmo, his half-leg hidden behind her puffed-out skirt to make him look normal. Roxanne hung it over the fireplace. I don't mean it as a criticism. I was glad for her. Though it made me look bad in a whole new way.

The other problem, even bigger than money, was me. I was in the middle of something I'd never wanted. For a while Roxanne had me talked into thinking I did want it or at least that I had wanted it but the truth was I didn't and never had. There were times that I liked it all right, but I didn't *want* it. There's a difference.

I talked to Jack about it one night when things were so bad between Roxanne and me early on, when the news first broke about Karen. I couldn't sleep and I went downstairs to sneak a drink—I was back at it already by then, and I kept a bottle in with the mixing bowls in the baking station in the pantry where I knew Roxanne would never go—and there was Jack at the kitchen table, playing solitaire.

So, I said, you up for a game? And she said sure and dealt me five cards. I won a hundred twenty dollars off her at poker that night and we sat up until three talking. I ended up telling her about Karen, the whole thing, more than I ever told Roxanne or the shrink. I even told her about the abortion. I suppose I shouldn't have said anything but I had no one else to talk to.

Roxanne hated me for that. Never forgave me. Of all the crappy things I did to her—I admit it, I did—that was the one she could not forgive. She had this thing with Jack, she always had to pretend to her her life was perfect even though it was obvious to everyone it was a complete mess. I didn't know that yet though. I'd thought her mother already knew about me, that she'd told her all about what a lowdown dirty dog I was because they were both women and that's just what they did, confide in each other about what assholes men are, but it turned out Roxanne was so busy trying to prove her life was better than her mother's that she hadn't told her a thing.

Not that Jack seemed surprised. That was when she said I didn't strike her as the kind of guy who should be married. *No offense,* she'd said, taking a drag before reshuffling the cards in that expert way she had, puffing up the deck and then letting the cards fall in a little soft-sounding cascade, *but why don't you just leave?* She'd exhaled and, from behind a cloud of smoke added, *she'd get over it.*

I was kind of shocked. I thought Roxanne's own mother would be on her side. *Tell Roxanne that,* I'd said, and she said *I plan to* and then we both laughed and she dealt another hand. I felt kind of guilty, though, laughing like that when Roxanne was upstairs crying. But it was a good question. Why didn't I just leave? Maybe I should have, that night even, but I didn't know where else to go.

"Go move in with what's her name," Jack had said in her gravelly voice, reading my mind as she slapped a fresh hand down on the table. I didn't want to say it but I didn't want to do that either. By then I was a little tired of Karen too. I was tired of women in general except for the fact that I kept ending up in bed with them.

It wasn't that I didn't love them, or some of them some of the time. I did. I love women. I just didn't love them the way they wanted me to. That was the thing I'd told Karen about Roxanne that I probably shouldn't have, the thing she seemed to understand until it turned out she didn't. She thought I meant I wanted her *instead of* Roxanne but really what I meant was that I wanted only part of both of them, at the same time, and only in small amounts, like if I added up the total of how much I wanted Karen and Roxanne and April in my life it would all have come to about sixty percent, and the rest of my time I'd rather have spent alone. Or with Val. I missed Val. Although I wasn't sure I wanted to get back with her either. But how do you tell a woman that, let alone two women or three and their mothers—by then Karen was pressuring me to meet her mother. And her grandmother. I guess it was wrong of me to take so long to admit that to Roxanne, about not really wanting to be with her. I should have told her sooner. Maybe I did *misrepresent my intentions*— that's what the shrink said—but by the time I told her I didn't want to be there it was too late. She was pregnant. I felt really bad about that, for her almost as much as for me.

Then May came along and everything changed. I changed. Sweet May, my chocolate bunny, my little brown bug. The thing about May was, at the beginning I didn't want her any more than I wanted the rest of it, but as soon as I had her I loved her. Even April, who I was crazy about—though she was increasingly less so about me by then—got on my nerves sometimes. But May was just sweetness. She was the only one who didn't ever hate me and that was only the beginning of why I loved her. Little Miss May, Maybelle as I called her.

May was the beginning of a whole new story. We were all she had. That's why I stayed. Though if you hear Roxanne tell it, I stayed for the free rent and the stainless steel self-cleaning six-burner convection oven.

I wrote a song about her, May, Maybelle, Mabel, as I like to call her, though only when Roxanne isn't around because she doesn't approve. *Mabel if you were able I'd take you to the prom. Mabel if I were able I'd introduce you to my Mom.* It goes on, it's a love song written in the voice of her first boyfriend, who's kind of a mess, and who's dying of love for her even though she's different from the other girls. In the song she's the cute one and he's longing for her.

I like to think she'll have a boyfriend like that some day, someone who's crazy about her. I like to think she'll talk and flirt and have lots of good sex. What kind of a father hopes his little daughter will grow up to have sex you say, but I did. I wanted her to snap out of her sad little funk and laugh and fall in love with someone, and not some two-timing half-assed jerk like me but a really nice guy, and grow up to be, well, normal.

MAY

On a damp Sunday afternoon on the first anniversary of the day I arrived, Roxanne gave a party in my honor. We were having the party, she said, because it was important to *celebrate life's passages.*

My sorry face was the party's motif. It appeared on the cover of the *Memory Book* Roxanne made afterward, a tome in which every detail of this blighted event is recorded. She kept it in the hall bookcase next to her scrapbook of April's school pictures—who knows where these things are now—and had the year printed on the book's spine as if this were the first of an annual series, though the party was a one-time event. The book stood out on the shelf after that, a fading anomaly of pink optimism among ratty disintegrating telephone books and tattered half-read novels.

Roxanne was a whirlwind of organizational energy that week, so hopeful. She'd put Craig on notice that everything had to be *perfect.* She'd designed an official-looking logo made up of my picture and the date of my inauspicious arrival surrounded with the words *Birth of a Family* written in ornate script and had this aesthetic atrocity printed on everything that would take ink, from coffee mugs to backpacks to paper plates and napkins, though the actual day the party commemorated was shadowed, for those of us who remembered, by sad or guilty memories. But what were mere facts to my mother? She'd rewritten history and insisted the day of my arrival was *the most beautiful day of her life.*

So that morning, while Grandma Jack mixed Hawaiian Punch and Orange Crush in a huge ice-filled bowl, and mixed up a second, stronger batch for her and Craig in a quart jar, and while Craig stood on a ladder stapling pink crepe paper to the garage, Roxanne sat at the kitchen table stuffing goodie bags with little packets of pink jellybeans, white leatherette New Testaments and rolled-up T-shirts printed with that glum-looking picture of me. My mother's idea, I believe, was to prove to the world that, despite appearances, things were working out.

She'd invited Pastor Gary, of course, and her Young Adoptive Parents' fellowship group and the parents and children from the South American adoption support group and the few neighbors we were still on speaking terms with. She'd ordered an enormous pink cake and three flavors of pink ice cream—strawberry, peppermint and cherry swirl—each in a gallon tub. Thirty-eight people showed up, including Golgotha, who played one set and then stopped because one of the neighbors who hadn't been invited called the police.

Phoebe came and brought the dogs—Bill, of course, and Lola, a blind Chow she was fostering, and Mr. Cosmo, who'd been staying with Phoebe so he wouldn't disrupt the preparations. Cosmo was so glad to be home and so excited by the food and the people he broke his not very sturdy retractable leash and ran laps around the backyard, knocking down several brown babies and straddling them on the ground to lick frosting off their faces.

About Mr. Cosmo and babies, in Mr. Cosmo's defense: he never meant them harm. Most of them cried when he knocked them down at the party that day, some just a little while others shrieked and sobbed, though none were hurt. Their parents scooped them up and comforted them, shooting glowering looks over their shoulders in Phoebe's direction, assuming he was hers. Some of them even left early because of him.

It never bothered me though, not that day or ever. I was seventeen months old by then and finally starting to walk. I was unsteady and it's true, his velocity, as he ran his lopsided laps around the perimeter of the yard, tipped me over, toppling stout little me, in my bright pink dress and matching socks, into the muddy grass. Even though I'd grown thick and solid by then I was still shaky on my too-small feet, even in the special sturdy shoes they'd bought me, but to be bumped to the ground and stood over by this silvery ghost of a dog didn't faze me at all.

I remember how he blocked the sun as he stared down at me that day with his worried yellow eyes, dangling his front left stump in my face and breathing his earthy hot dog-scented breath all over me. When he lowered his wide pink tongue to collect cake crumbs from my cheek his touch felt gentle, like a warm rough washcloth daubed by a trustworthy mother. To lie there under him felt safe and deeply consoling and entirely natural to me and I was sorry to be rescued by some efficient and outraged stranger.

Since that first glance we'd exchanged on the day Roxanne brought me home we'd had an understanding. I'd never feared him or any dog. I knew he'd never hurt me and he believed the same of me. I agreed with Phoebe, though of course we'd never discussed it. Any dog was better company than almost any human being.

PHOEBE

Every morning after I walk the dogs and before I start my work I make a pot of tea—it used to be coffee but my stomach can't handle it anymore—and I carry the tea on a tray, along with a small pitcher of milk and three glucosamine tablets, into my office and start to settle in. I plan my work for the day, easing into it slowly. First, I make a to-do list on a lined index card. Then I look over the manuscript I'm working on, stir the papers on my desk, rearrange the Post-it notes stuck to my computer, read my notes from the night before and try to collect my thoughts.

I'm a textbook editor. I work from home for a company in a nearby suburb, editing middle school textbooks mostly, sometimes high school. Occasionally I write articles for these books, but mostly I just edit them. Sometimes I compile anthologies for literature texts and this is the work I like best. But mostly what I do is fact and grammar checking, content screening, *language smoothing*, as my boss insists on calling it. I specialize in what they call the softer subjects, social studies mainly. American history, government, sociology, beginning psychology and something they call values education. This work usually goes well and any tweaking I do, even when it comes to content, goes largely unnoticed.

My job is difficult only in so much as the books I edit are boring. The language is so attenuated, so bland and careful, as to be almost unreadable. I used to try to beef it up and boil it down, but my boss told me to leave it alone so now I only correct the errors and leave the style as is.

Wherever I can, just to relieve the boredom, I try to slip in original documents—The Bill of Rights, for instance, or The

Gettysburg Address. I particularly like to add this second one, which I had to memorize in seventh grade but which children now seem never to have heard of. At 272 words it doesn't even take up a full page. In the little box I get to write to go alongside it I'd like to say that if they read only one thing in the book this should be it. I'd like to tell them to imagine the seven thousand corpses dragged off the battlefield at Gettysburg and say that it took Abraham Lincoln two minutes to deliver the speech after a two-hour oration by someone named Edward Everett that no one remembers. I'd like to ask them to consider this if they're ever invited to give a speech in memory of the dead, as some of them likely will be one day. I'd like to tell them to keep it short, out of respect for the silence of the grave.

But I don't. What I say instead in my allotted fifty words is that presidents used to write their own speeches and that this is one of the best. The writers of these books, though, are no Lincolns, and it is their very verbosity that keeps me in work.

It is my editing of the language arts books—the ones meant to introduce children to poetry, fiction, drama, mythology—that gets me into trouble. These earnest-sounding books with their vague, alliterative titles—*Language and Literature for Young Learners, Pathways through Prose and Poetry* or, as I like to think of it, *Passionate Pokes through Puberty*—beg for spicing up. I long to plant bombs of sex and death in the bland little chapters, not to harm the children but to confirm that what they suspect is true. Pain, fear, love, lust, pride, hate, shame, spite, death—these are life's real themes, not any of the multi-syllabic abstractions these books so confusingly go on about. But my opinions are strictly not allowed. The text is there to point away from all that, to point to *Morals and Meanings*, as one title so pompously puts it, to blunt the sheer vertigo-inducing effects of *Language and Literature*, as if to quell some anticipated disturbance in an incendiary population—prisoners, for instance, or mental patients. It's not quite censorship, just officiousness, and I'm dying to stamp it out, to restore to these stories their dangerousness.

But I don't get to touch these chapters now. After a few attempts I was told to stop. My opportunity for influence comes later, at the end of each book. Here, untainted by editorial comment, are the recommended reading lists and mostly overlooked anthologies of poems and stories deemed appropriate for children aged eleven through fourteen.

My job is to read this material closely for *upsetting, disturbing or age-inappropriate subject matter or language.* When I find it I'm supposed to notify my boss and provide a recommendation for something more innocuous to take its place. Trouble is, we don't agree on what is appropriate, though I have the company's Taste Guidelines Manual in my possession, somewhere, and am expected to follow its recommendations.

The first time a problem arose was when I replaced the somewhat insipid, I always thought, *Annabel Lee* with the far juicier *The Fall of the House of Usher* as the single Edgar Allan Poe entry in *Anthems and Allegories: An Anthology of American Literature.* My boss called me from home at nine-thirty at night to complain.

"What were you thinking?" he'd said, in a tone that was supposed to be humorous. This was not long after Duane died and my boss was still trying not to upset me. I had no idea what he was talking about at first. What twelve-year-old wouldn't rather read a story about burying your sister alive than some rhyming jingle about an old girlfriend, even if she was dead?

"It's insipid," I'd said, too drunk to lie. "We might as well print the lyrics to *Teen Angel.*" I'd had three glasses of wine with dinner. Actually I'd had them instead of dinner. I didn't feel like mincing words. "Those pounding rhymes," I went on. "They give me a headache. 'Can ever dissever.' Please. "

"I know this material may be difficult for you, Phoebe," my boss said, in his trying-to-sound-kind voice, "but please try to be objective. Children enjoy rhyming poetry. They enjoy innocent love stories."

What they enjoy more is someone getting buried alive, I thought.

"And there's the problem of the language," he continued in his shocked-sounding way. "Do you really think twelve-year-olds, even gifted ones, are likely to know the meaning of words like ennui? Trepidation?"

Who cares, I thought—or did I say it?—lying down on my bed and letting the phone fall away from my ear. *Don't the little brats own dictionaries?*

I felt the phone being jostled from my hand. "Good point," said the puppet in her most perfect diction. She had appeared out of nowhere. "I see what you mean," she was saying sincerely into the phone.

Though dormant for years she had become active since the funeral and lately elbowed me from the phone whenever she sensed trouble. Now she was standing on my chest, the hem of her starchy little dress covering my mouth. I could hardly breath. Still, the phone was at my ear—we seemed to share an ear—and I could hear my boss panting on the other end of the line. What was he doing? I could hear the sound of manuscript pages being riffled. I pictured him in his bathrobe sitting on the edge of the toilet, behind his locked bathroom door, his grimy briefcase leaning against the bathtub as he hid from his screaming children and the drone of the television that filled his small house. Not that I'd ever been there.

"Though that's not even the main point," my boss was saying, forging ahead, trying to maintain his air of patient disappointment in the face of the puppet's sudden, implacable charm. "What about these disturbing phrases, this 'morbid acuteness of the senses'? What is a child to make of that? Or the not-so-subtle suggestion of incest and live burial? Or the mention of opium in the first paragraph? My goodness, Phoebe, really. Do you really think that's appropriate for twelve-year-olds?"

Sure, I tried to say. *That's just the kind of thing they like.* He heard nothing though. The puppet had my mouth covered with her little wooden hands.

"Phoebe, I'm going to have to overrule you this time. No hard feelings, I hope. I know you're not quite yourself yet."

"Thank you. I understand completely," the puppet me said. "And have a nice evening." She smiled at me and clacked her little wooden teeth together as she hung up the phone. *Annabel Lee* stayed.

The next time I got a call from my boss about my questionable judgment it concerned my decision to include a certain passage from *To Kill a Mockingbird*.

"Oh come on," I'd said, mumbling into the starchy doll's dress the puppet usually wore, which she had ripped off and stuffed into my mouth as a gag the minute she heard the phone ring. *That book is beyond reproach* I was trying to say.

"I laud your decision to include this wonderful book, Phoebe, but I'm distressed that you have chosen the one sexual passage from its entirety to represent what is otherwise a wholesome and uplifting story of moral courage and triumph."

I managed to spit out most of the dress. "What?" I said.

"I am referring to your inclusion of the passage containing the phrase, and please forgive me but I quote, 'ruttin' on my Mayella.' Phoebe. Did it ever occur to you that such an objectionable locution may frighten young female readers or even,"—here he lowered his voice—"confusingly arouse young boys? Did it ever occur to you that it conflicts with our editorial policy of a wholesome approach to sex education with an emphasis on respect and consensual mutual pleasure, an approach that is at the heart of our educational policy?"

The guy who says that is the villain I tried to say.

"Phoebe did you ever even read the TGM? I sent you the most recent revision last October."

TGM. For a moment I was at a loss. The Tale of the Grimacing Marionette? The Totally Grandiose Midget? The Terrible Gooey Melanoma? Then I remembered. The Taste Guidelines Manual.

"Of course I've read it," the puppet was saying. "It's very helpful. Thank you for sending it."

"Good. Then you understand how disturbing this might be," he said.

I wanted to point out that children's lives are full of disturbances, that they might find the subject useful. Instead the puppet agreed that my boss had made yet another *good point* and hung up as soon as possible.

For a while after that my boss watched my work very closely. When nothing unusual showed up for a while he relaxed, figuring I'd come to my senses, believing he'd won the moral high ground. But when the coast seemed clear, I reverted to my old ways. I slipped a few Joyce Carol Oates stories into my recommendation lists and when those went unnoticed I added an excerpt from *The Bell Jar* to an anthology. Nothing. It wasn't until he discovered I'd included a passage from *Lolita* concerning the exchange of money for certain particularly choice sexual favors in a new anthology called *Coming of Age* that I heard from him again.

"Phoebe, this isn't even remotely funny if that's what you're thinking," my boss was saying in another of his postprandial phone calls from the toilet, no longer sounding humorous or even patient. I could hear his shaky voice bouncing off the tile walls. "I'm assuming this is some kind of tasteless joke, to prove I actually read these submissions of yours? Unless it's a total lack of judgment on your part. Frankly, I don't know what's worse."

Fortunately I was way back in the cave that night, sitting in the dark, hog-tied, tongue-tied and liquored up, and couldn't even get to the phone, let alone form complete sentences. The puppet handled everything. She apologized, even cried a little, and at the end, as always, thanked him.

So I never got the chance to say I'd meant it. But I did. Lo belonged there, right there in the *Coming of Age* anthology, lowdown Lo, vulgar little Lo with her brains and her broken heart and that beautiful tennis serve. Now there's a real girl, I thought, a girl our readers could relate to, a girl exactly their age who knew almost as much about fellatio as they did.

It was a lost cause though. I never made a dent. I always got caught. I began to think the only way to get to girls wasn't to infiltrate my boss's textbooks but to compile one of my own.

I even had a title, *Write On Real Girls!*, though I couldn't imagine who would publish what I had in mind. My idea was that each chapter would be dedicated to one girl from fiction or history. Chapter One would be Lolita. Chapter Two would be Frankie from *The Member of the Wedding*; Chapter Three would be Scout from *To Kill a Mockingbird*. Chapter Four, Alice from *Alice in Wonderland*. Chapter Five, vain doomed Connie from that Joyce Carol Oates story, almost too old at fifteen but too disastrously real to leave out. Chapter Six, Anne Frank, unabridged, from before her father edited out the parts about sex. After that I wasn't sure—there were so many. Pecola, Esperanza, Nancy Drew. Maybe even Pollyanna.

I thought about changing the title to *The Slumber Party* and writing the closing chapter myself. Actually I'd already started it as a one-act play. I imagined them all gathering for a slumber party, a sleepover as they call it these days. Every girl would arrive with something she liked to eat and stay to tell her story. Lo would bring potato chips and brag about blowjobs. Alice would bring jam tarts and talk about why girls should study math. I'd be the hostess, discreetly removing myself to the top of the basement stairs to eavesdrop and wait for the pizza delivery. Imagine what they'd have to say to each other, after all those caffeinated soft drinks I planned to serve.

I know I'm mixing fact and fiction. But isn't that what life is? Isn't that what you get when you add up what happened with what you imagine happened, which, after you think about it long enough, is at least as real? I think the play needs to be written, though I haven't told anyone about it yet. Once, late at night, when the puppet was safely asleep, I Googled teenage heroines to see if there was anyone I was forgetting, and Google, prompt and polite as always, replied *Did you mean: teenage heroes?* No, I did not.

My point exactly.

The next time my boss called it was to say my job had been *reclassified* and that I was now a *generalist* and would not be working on any more anthologies but would continue to specialize in social studies. "Ah," I said, not understanding except that there had been another reduction in my duties, another demotion as a result of my continued lack of cooperation in enforcing *language standards,* though my pay, he said, would remain the same. I was meant to be insulted. "I understand, thank you for calling," said the puppet, always expert at making conversation in an awkward moment. "Have a nice day," she said as she hung up.

So now I'm a specialist in generalities I imagined saying to Duane. Duane would have laughed the whole thing off. *That guy's a gen-u-wine walking talking oxyfuckinmoron-maker* he would have said. Sometimes I imagine things he would have said, so much so now that I'm starting to forget what he really did say. Being alone is too much freedom for someone with sliding standards of honesty like me. Sometimes I think I've made him up to be better than he was. I'm afraid I'm starting to invent him as I wished he'd been. Lately I've noticed there's a second puppet hanging around, a folksy foulmouthed Duane puppet that gooses the me puppet when she's asleep and speaks for Duane from the grave. Not that it matters, now that he's gone.

I ease into my day. Once I start editing a manuscript I have to keep going to keep the tone in my head, so before I begin I indulge myself a little. I read my email, I read my horoscope, I check my bank balance though I have no reason to believe it's any different than it was the day before. I check out Zoo Cam and watch a panda bear munch endlessly in the middle of a pile of bamboo. I read the weather forecast in distant cities I don't plan to visit.

I am edging toward what I really want, the highlight of my day, the CNN news. Or rather the news headlines, twenty pregnant lines that sketch a weird contour of a weirder world at that particular moment. I take my time to read each one, savoring every word as I try to unpack each headline's dense meaning, on guard for surprising connections. Each is like a puzzle, a poem. Every word merits contemplation, suggests many possible meanings. Each line signifies some change of fortune, large or small, a cataclysm, a tragedy, a failure, a decision or very occasionally a boon. Each is an epiphany in six or seven words. Each is an omen that predicts my day.

Beautiful person died on hospital floor

I linger over each word as if parsing the Torah. Was it the person's beauty that died on the floor that day, or was it her—I assume her, else why the word beautiful?—sense of herself as beautiful, dead perhaps from the humiliation of being on the floor, which, when she stood up, was gone? Or does it mean that an actual physical body, which was beautiful, fell on the floor and died? Is this obvious to everyone but me, or is it meant to confuse?

When I get to the bottom of the list I start over and if I think I can stand it I'll choose one story and click. The best ones balance thrill against revulsion and keep me on edge between the two. Most end badly, though sometimes I'm surprised by the flat landing of a happy ending, even a little disappointed that things aren't as bad as I was led to believe. But these are exceptions and more often the stories are, if not simply horrific, at least bittersweet, containing some indissolvable stone of pain that seems meant to remind the reader that we must pay for our happy endings.

After the dolphin led the child to shore she couldn't find her way out of the bay and died, leaving her own calf motherless. The woman withdrew from the window ledge and was embraced by her husband who forgave her indiscretion with the fireman only to learn she was leaving them both for her lawyer. After the miners were rescued their boss announced he was laying them off. Sure, sometimes a lost dog made his way home after years. But now he was old. He'd lost his playfulness and was gray around the muzzle. Soon he would die. There were no happy endings, really.

I bought a speckled black notebook and began to write the headlines down. When I filled up one, I bought another. I was on my seventh.

I glance outside, momentarily surprised to see that it's a summer day. It's still early, before the heat gets ugly and the light makes your head hurt. There are red berries on a branch outside my office window. I pause to watch as a fat brown bird lands on the branch and rotates one beady eye in my direction before he opens his beak and closes it over one berry, tugs and then flits off. The dappled light on the driveway camouflages the neighbor's white and gray cat, Pike, who has slipped through the broken boards of my fence to lie there in my driveway in a milky, honeyed ecstasy. He appears melted, stretching himself flat on the pavement, surrendering to the heat. For just a moment I think I might break out, do the unthinkable and go out to pet him. Maybe take him a sardine and kneel there in broad daylight in the driveway as he eats it. But then I don't. I look back to my grayish screen and to the headlines there and the soft sunny vision disappears.

Here are the headlines for the first day I began writing them down.

House to apologize for slavery
62,000 jobs lost in June
Missing Vermont girl found dead
Bombers want to be beheaded not shot to death
Students tortured, stabbed to death
Man sells soul for $3800 . . . to pizza joint
Ranch salad dressing floods basement
PETA tells military stop burning shooting goats
Cyber affairs can be cause for divorce
Dead girl taken for sex ring
Ideas for wayward dolphins: scare, coax, trap
Husband convicted in wife's anti-freeze death
Wildfire evacuations ordered at Big Sur
Gas hits new high in time for holiday travel
Don't let a natural disaster ruin your vacation

This last caught my attention, if only for the jauntiness of its tone. Did it simply mean to advise vacationing families to avoid the tropics during hurricane season? Or did it suggest something more intriguing, that it was possible to enjoy one's vacation *in spite* of a natural disaster, in the midst of one, even? Which begged an even larger question. What was a natural disaster, anyway? Did it have to be geologic? Atmospheric? Or did discontent count? Sorrow, strife? Wasn't the term itself redundant? What was more natural than disaster? I refreshed my screen. The headline had already changed.

How to survive a natural disaster

I read the list every day. It was an astringent, like splashing cold water on your face. Once I read that French women kept their breasts beautiful by splashing cold water on them every morning and I'd tried it for a month, but it didn't make any difference. I was young then, my breasts were already beautiful and when they stopped being beautiful an ocean of ice water couldn't save them. I suppose the idea was that shock made your skin tighten. My father used to splash cold water on his face before he left for work in the morning, maybe to prepare for the assaults of the day, to throw cold water on himself before the world could. That's what this was like—an immersion in the cold water of reality before going out to face the day. Although, of course, I did not do that, go out that is. Why bother when it was all online and none of it was good.

Pekinese inherits fortune, son sues

I remember when this sort of thing seemed funny, ages ago, before I could imagine how the son felt, how the dying man felt, before I could imagine the years of slights and escalating insults, the simple comfort of a dog. Now it scares me, though I can't look away. I remember when I was young, when people who were the age that I am now said they didn't watch the evening news because it scared them. I thought they were exaggerating, boasting. I thought they meant to prove how tenderhearted they were or maybe, I thought, it was a figure of speech, like when people said *I was so embarrassed I could have died* or *if you do that again I'll kill you*.

But now I understand they meant it, all of it. Now the news scares me, and sometimes headlines are all I can stand. Sometimes I can't even stand those. There was one so terrible the other day I didn't even write it down. I try not to think about the ones about animals unless they're humorous.

Escaped giraffe steals tot's treat, naps standing

That's about my speed. I scroll down for more but there's no more levity.

Heat wave temps to soar, elder deaths expected
Dwindling penguins signal ocean woes

As much as I hate the news, I love the headlines, the way they're written. Headline writers, copy editors, are the poets of the everyday. I don't mean me and my fussy little textbooks. I mean Duane. That's what he did—twenty-eight years on the graveyard shift at the *Chicago Sun-Times*, back when they still had copy editors, before they bought the old ones out with early retirement and fired the young ones, back before they settled for spell-check and everyone stopped buying the paper. Back when headline writing was an art. Duane was good.

It's all changed now. Too bad they don't use those good old tabloid words much anymore—like *slay*. Duane always said a good headline rode on its verb. I do like how CNN compresses a story into a few words. I like the rigor of it. Every word has weight. Duane would have liked *Dwindling penguins signal ocean woes*. He would have liked *signal*.

After I started to copy the headlines I couldn't stop. I had to do it every morning. Frankly, I thought there was some hidden message for me there, maybe sent from Duane, which, once I figured it out, would allow me to—what? I don't know exactly, but change somehow. Relax, get back on track. It got out of control for a while, I admit. The headlines kept changing and it became an all-day thing, searching for the hidden meanings and writing them down. My work suffered. I had to cut back.

Now I just write down the first twenty headlines and close out the site. It takes self-control but it pays off the next morning when I see which stories have legs. Duane's newspaper lingo that, *legs*. Other stories disappear in minutes never to return. What happened to the twenty-year-old Russian supermodel who *plunged to her death* from the window of a Manhattan hotel room, the one with the broad shoulders and impossibly high cheekbones who the publicist said *had a face from a fairy tale*? I never found out. The story disappeared in a day.

Sex sting snags world's greatest dad

Some days though I can't wait to see how a story develops, as if the only defense against its terribleness is to know what happened next. It doesn't make sense but on days like those I check the headlines hourly. Like today. I go back to see what's changed and these have been added:

Dead Vermont girl's uncle faces kidnap charges
American Airlines cuts 7,000 jobs
Baby for sale on eBay goes home

A baby goes home. It's a good note to end on. Though I worry. What kind of home did that baby go home to? But I'm powerless to affect the outcome and I close the window and get to work. Today I'm editing a chapter on teen depression.

CRAIG

Gary agreed to counsel us—no charge—on one condition: that I stop seeing Karen. I agreed, sort of, until he made me sign a contract. It was full of all kinds of crap about respect and communication. Loyalty, truth, compromise, reconciliation. Forgiveness. And love of course. I was supposed to sign a binding contract to love. *Read Corinthians* he kept saying, as if I hadn't, like that was really going to help me sort out my sex life. It made me want to break it just to spite him. In my opinion Gary is not only a pompous hypocritical narcissistic prick, he had a thing for Roxanne even then. But I went along with it to please her, or I tried to, except for the part about not seeing Karen.

PHOEBE

There's one more thing I should tell you.

I found him. Duane that is. This is years ago now, before I met Roxanne, though sometimes it seems like yesterday. I found him in the garage, hanging by his neck. Kicked-away ladder on the floor below. Hardware store bag with the receipt for the rope still in his car. Also, still in the bag, was the anti-itch dog shampoo I'd asked him to buy. Later, when I found the receipt, I was surprised to see the rope was so cheap. It was a good buy. Get it? I think it was a message, Duane's last joke, in lieu of the note he didn't write. Or which he wrote and I failed to find. I'm still looking. It's one of a number of reasons I can't move.

I was surprised, not that he'd done it, but how. I was surprised he was able to, that he knew how to tie the right knot and tie it tight enough and high enough in the rafters. He was never particularly handy. I imagined what our life would have been like after, if he had tried and failed, if the knot had slipped, or the rope had been too long, if his feet had brushed the ground and he'd had to stand there on his toes and wait to be rescued. I imagined how embarrassed he'd have been and us laughing about it, much later as he finally died of the other thing, the disease. I picture him lying in a hospital bed pulling his hospital gown away from the rope burn scar. *Ow,* he'd have said. *Close call. Ha.*

I found him early on a Saturday morning. I was going to my yoga class, back when I still bothered with that sort of thing. He hadn't been in bed when I woke up but he often wasn't. He was pretty sick by then, and I'd thought he'd probably fallen asleep in the guest room where he'd gone to read so he wouldn't wake me up. I stood at the kitchen window and hit the garage door remote button and watched, as I used to enjoy doing, as the humming door lifted like a theater curtain. I expected to see the back of my car. Instead I saw Duane's feet, barely eighteen inches from the ground. Bedroom slippers dangling from dirty white socks, swinging slightly. The window was open and I heard the hum of the door as it continued its upward motion. Next I saw a pair of stained gray sweat pants, then his hands, looking dark and already swollen, then the tails of his green plaid flannel shirt, and then as the door reached the top and slid curving into its slot, I saw the thinning hair on the back of Duane's head, which was bent at that ridiculous angle, like the punch line of some joke he would have acted out.

Later I heard that people thought I was cold. Some official person—the ambulance driver? I'd called an ambulance though it was hours too late—asked *Was your husband suffering from depression, ma'am?* and I said *apparently.* Or so I was told. I don't remember.

PART TWO

CRAIG

It all started—I mean my so-called art career—when I won a contest in seventh grade. I won first place in the Annual Thomas Jefferson Junior High School Art Fair. I even beat out all the eighth graders, the first time that had ever happened in the sixteen years they'd held the contest. The grand prize was a one-year scholarship for unlimited classes at the Scottsdale Art Center—drawing, painting, pottery, photography, stained glass, glass blowing, jewelry, anything you wanted although all I wanted to do was draw—and a gift certificate for free art supplies. It was a big deal, not just the scholarship but the recognition.

Everybody expected Kenny Lindner to win, especially Kenny, and when he didn't it changed both our lives. I still remember our entries, his and mine, in their buckled mats, and how they looked on easels on the school stage. Mine had a big blue ribbon on it; Kenny's ribbon was smaller and red. He'd entered what seemed at the time like a perfect copy of a magazine photo of some pop singer everyone had a hard-on for that year. I can't remember her name. Some blonde with big boobs and a bare shoulder. It was good, like everything he did, but pretty risqué for junior high, and the judges, a bunch of old ladies including Miss Vosanelik, our art teacher, didn't like it. They didn't like him. I entered a drawing of my grandfather, who'd died earlier that year. I copied a photo too, but I added little vignettes of his life in the sky around him like thought bubbles. Corny as hell. It was my mother's idea. It wasn't as good as Kenny's, but it was more original, or would have been if I'd thought of it myself. I suppose they went for sentiment. They also just liked me better. Women usually did.

120

I ran into Kenny in a bar in Phoenix a few years ago, on a trip home, after my father's first heart attack. The bar was down the street from the hospital, dark and over air-conditioned in the middle of the bright hot day. I'd needed a break from the ICU and sneaked away, and there was Kenny, alone on a bar-stool at three in the afternoon, wearing a pale green linen suit and cowboy boots, drinking a glass of Chardonnay. He was completely bald, shaved I think. He recognized me, not the other way around. He'd always been a big kid but now he was huge, two-eighty at least.

"Well, damn. Could that be Craig Dahlberg, the famous artist?" he'd said, when I sat down. It took me a minute to figure out who he was.

We shot the shit for a while. He told me about his life or at least the parts he wanted me to know. Three *terrific* kids. A wife that taught aerobics—he winked—his own ad agency. Life was *terrific*. No explanation for why he was alone in a bar at three in the afternoon. Dressed like that. He said I should *feel free* to get in touch with him if I ever needed a job. Maybe he was bullshitting but maybe not. Maybe I should have taken him up on it. I looked him up later; he really did have his own agency.

"Man, could you draw," he said, clinking his wine glass against my beer.

"Not like you," I said.

"Whatever," he said, not disagreeing. He laughed, showing off a mouth full of eerily white teeth. "Man, you have no idea what that did to me."

"What?" I said, embarrassed. I hoped he wasn't remembering how I'd brown-nosed the head judge. I'd complimented her on her hair.

"Water under the bridge," he said, motioning for the bartender to send over another drink for me. "Never could have made it as a real artist. Not like you, you skinny little prick!" He punched my shoulder.

I've been thinking about Kenny lately. About how he lost, but maybe in the long run he won. That's the thing about early success. More bad than good comes of it, usually. When you lose you feel like shit but you move on. It's harder when you win—you feel like shit later, if you don't live up to it. And how can you? One perfect day and it's all downhill from there.

Or maybe it's just me. Winning that contest was the high point of my life, and I was twelve. It was even better than when I got the scholarship to Chicago. I'm not even sure I wanted to go. By then everyone just expected it and I was more worried about the embarrassment of not getting in than I was excited when I did. They shouldn't do that to kids. Turn everything into a contest, I mean. Set up some ultimate something and make everything and everyone else seem like second best. Like with April, and May.

Anyway, about Roxanne, we really did try to work it out. For the sake of the girls. And not just for a while. For seven years we tried everything we could to maintain some kind of family life, for them. At first we tried to go back to what Roxanne called *a normal life,* whatever that is. When that didn't work we tried living apart-but-together. I moved to the spare room over the garage and kept my basement studio. I still used the kitchen when Roxanne wasn't around, and we officially *saw other people.* Then I moved in with Karen—she took me back on the condition that I promise to stop lying and drinking—but I kept my studio at Roxanne's. Then Karen threatened to kick me out because I was at Roxanne's all the time. I tried to tell her I was just there working. And cooking, which was how I paid my studio rent and how I got to see the girls and Jack, but Karen didn't believe I wasn't there to see Roxanne.

Karen didn't understand. Roxanne and I could barely stand the sight of each other. But I loved my girls. And I loved that kitchen. Every Saturday morning I'd go over and cook for the week. I'd make spaghetti sauce and meatloaf and corn bread and a big pot of some kind of soup or stew and May would sit on the floor and watch me cook and April would run through on her way to some lesson and before I left I'd put out a big plate of scraps for Mr. Cosmo. It felt good. Useful. If there was enough I'd bring some home for us in Tupperware bowls.

"I can't eat this," she'd say when she was mad at me. We were always having the same fight.

"What's wrong with it?" I'd say, pretending I thought I'd put too much garlic in the sauce.

"It makes me sick that you're there all the time," she'd say.

"It's the only way I get to see my kids," I'd say.

"No it's not," she'd say. "You could bring them here, cook for them here."

I couldn't though; Roxanne wouldn't let me. Besides, Karen had an electric stove. After a few months she went on a hunger strike, refusing to eat what I cooked unless I cooked it there with her. It drove me crazy. She got thinner and thinner, ate nothing but hummus and licorice, just to spite me. This isn't normal, I said, you have to eat. Fuck you, she said, and threw me out. Roxanne's Tupperware is still there.

So I moved back to my room over the garage. My stuff was everywhere. I still had clothes in the back of a closet in Roxanne's bedroom, stuff at Karen's, unless she threw it all out, a closet full of stuff in Roxanne's garage, my whole studio in Roxanne's basement, plus two duffel bags full of clothes I'd left at my parents' when I moved back there for a couple of months. Phoebe had my potter's wheel on her screened porch under a pile of newspapers. One of my guitars and an accordion I'd bought at a flea market were still in Austin, at Val's, and I started keeping clothes at Jack's for emergencies. She didn't have a spare closet so I kept them piled in a cardboard box in the basement until they started to mildew. After that they just sat in a pile in a corner of the living room next to the TV.

"You can stay here for a while," she'd said, when I dropped in on her after one of my fights with Karen. "As long as you don't bring home any of your little chickies."

"Any of my little what?" I'd said, kissing the top of her balding gray head and pretending not to understand. It was nice of her to offer though. In fact it was almost a solution. In some ways those were the best times, with Jack. After I cleaned up the kitchen—an old fifties galley-style with a serviceable four-burner gas stove she never used—her place wasn't bad.

I'd pick up the girls and Mr. Cosmo and bring them over on Saturday afternoon and we'd cook dinner and have slumber parties when Roxanne went on dates. One time I pitched a tent in the living room and we all got inside and played poker. April was a natural. Or I should say the three of us played. May curled up against Mr. Cosmo and watched.

"Aren't you getting a little old for this," Jack said to me one night when I was rolling my sleeping bag out on her couch. May was sitting on the floor staring out the window at a cat. It was only the three of us that night. April had a sleepover with one of her girlfriends, but even when it was just me and May I always let her take the spare room.

I'd made pizza dough earlier in the day and had just spread sauce and Jack was putting pepperoni and mushroom slices on it the way I'd told her to. She handled the slices like poker chips.

"Just close your eyes and stick a pin in a map, if you have to," she was saying, slamming the sausage down artlessly. "Just pick something. A job, a city, hell, a closet." She made each option correspond to one slammed-down pepperoni slice. "You'd be surprised how one thing leads to another."

"That's what I'm afraid of," I'd said. I supposed she was right, though.

Finally I just went back to Roxanne, by default I guess. More of my stuff was there than anywhere else. Besides, I missed the kids. Especially May, but April too.

April never had been a calm child and I suppose our problems didn't help. When she was nine, when things got really rough between Roxanne and me, or rather when things got really rough again, Roxanne thought it would be a good idea to send her to stay with Drake in Connecticut for a few months. By then he'd remarried and he and his wife had three kids, Drake III, or *Tres* as they called him, and the girls, Brace and Whitman. But April had trouble there, too, and when she came back she was even more excitable, more *intense*, as her teacher put it, than she was before she left. Then Drake was transferred to Hong Kong, though he got his company to fly him to Chicago every couple of months, for meetings.

They kept a suite at the Four Seasons and she'd stay with him there, in her own little room with a canopy bed. I picked her up once and she showed it to me. There was a little table next to her bed with a silver hot chocolate pot on it and a half-eaten plate of pink-frosted shortbread cookies. She came home once wearing an Hermès scarf from the hotel gift shop. She told us she'd charged it to his room. She was ten.

On weekends he took her to his parents' place in Lake Forest, where they kept her horse, Charlie. Sometimes she stayed there all week. Elizabeth would take her out of school for shopping trips in the city and to meet Drake for lunch, then bring her back to us on Sunday night after dropping Drake at the airport. April would be carrying shopping bags and wearing her new clothes, a miniature Burberry raincoat once or a string of pearls, talking about the box seats they'd had at the opera. It drove Roxanne crazy. She took Elizabeth aside once and said, "Can you tone it down a little? How do you think this makes May feel?" Elizabeth had reached out one bony arm in the direction of April, who'd been listening, and pulled her back to lean against her chest. She'd wrapped her long arms around her favorite grandchild.

"Whatever you say, dear," she'd said in that tight-jawed way of hers, smoothing April's bright hair behind her ears. "But one of these days you'll see for yourself. Blood is thicker than water."

That's around the time April began to imitate Elizabeth's speech, smiling at us in that same disapproving way, using words like *ex*quisite to describe everything in her life away from us, hitting that first syllable hard to let us know how out of our league she was.

In those days May was the easy one. Quiet, compliant. Chunky, dark and still, like a beautiful carved stone. Though she was strange, I admit. When the time came for her to talk, she just didn't. When you spoke to her she'd look away, hiding behind that thick brush of black lashes as if speech were an embarrassment and she was waiting for you to stop. And she didn't do other things children did. She didn't play, didn't laugh.

She'd just stare when people asked her age, like she didn't understand the concept, though I saw her once when she was four counting out her stubby little fingers at her side, where she thought no one could see—one, two, three, four. She was secretive, stubborn. I didn't care. It made me love her more. It was our little secret that she wasn't stupid. I understood—she was biding her time. Somehow I knew that behind those black little eyes and inside that thick, still little body was a beautiful intelligent girl I would someday be able to talk to, a girl who was waiting to come out. I always believed in her. It may sound strange, but she reminded me of myself.

Roxanne worried, of course. She took her to doctors. She read up on her *condition*, on what she thought it might be. Everyone said to be patient, she was just slow, she'd been malnourished, she'd catch up. Then when she didn't, we got used to it. At five she was as silent as ever and so solitary. Her best and only real friend was Mr. Cosmo. He slept in her bed with his head on her pillow.

She was small for her age so we kept her out of school a year, but at six, when she still wasn't talking, we enrolled her in kindergarten.

"She's a little shy," I said to the teacher the first day, when I brought her in, dressed in her new blue jean jacket and denim skirt and matching yellow T-shirt and gym shoes. It might be a whole new beginning, I thought, leading her to the classroom door. But she wouldn't look at Mrs. Fields, a calm, wide, smiling woman who at least seemed kind. Instead she stared past her, toward a bowl of cloudy water on a side table where a depressed-looking goldfish swam in slow circles.

"She likes animals," I told Mrs. Fields. "Don't you?" I said to May, wagging one of her ponytails as if I expected a response.

"Isn't that nice," said Mrs. Fields, taking May's tiny brown hand in her big pink one and leading her away.

After Mrs. Fields got the kids settled she made us, the parents, leave. Fourteen young mothers and I stood in the hall and watched through a window for a while. Some of the mothers dabbed away tears prettily and finally all of them left but me. For an hour I watched as May sat and then lay, inert, with her skirt hiked up and her underpants showing, all alone on her little purple rug, the one I'd bought for her at Target weeks before, while the other kids cried and yelled and ran around and threw toys. There was a small fistfight, some vomit, a bathroom accident, many tears.

May didn't engage with any of it. I saw the teacher lead her to a small table and sit her down on a miniature chair and hand her paper and crayons. I saw how she picked up an orange crayon and started to draw a circle. Heart-piercing pride—my girl's an artist!—and then I watched as a fat blonde pig of a boy grabbed the crayon out of her hand—on the first day of school— and I saw how she didn't cry. Didn't protest, didn't kick, didn't grab it back, just tightened her little jaw in a gesture so small nobody but me would have noticed.

I wanted to flatten the kid, flatten the teacher for not doing anything and I tried to go in but the door was locked and so I banged on the window and the teacher came and told me that my behavior was unacceptable and I said but what are you going to do about that little shit, that menace, that little bully over there and she said children have to learn to work these things out on their own and I said let me talk to that little cocksucking brat a minute and she said that I had to leave or she'd call security.

Two weeks later Roxanne and I were called into a meeting and advised that May was being *assessed*. After a month we were told she was being transferred to a *special needs school*. She wasn't *thriving* we were told. She needed to be sent to a place where she *would thrive*. Roxanne called doctors and psychiatrists and lawyers who all agreed it was the right thing to do.

They said we were lucky to live in a place that had such a school. So after that, every morning I walked May to the corner where a special bus picked her up and took her to a special school in the next town.

In the beginning I rode the bus with her every morning but after a few days they told me to stop. They said it was better for her to learn independence. I could tell they thought that whatever was wrong with her was my fault, that her refusal to speak, if that's what it was, was the result of some terrible thing I'd done. I hated them for that but it didn't matter. Their opinion of me was just another nuisance to be endured if it would help her. But seeing her sitting in that seat all alone every morning, buttoned into her little hooded orange sweater with leaves embroidered on it—it was October by then—with her little hands lying still in her lap on top of her lime green vinyl backpack, so small and alone and not protesting, just letting herself be taken away, did something to me, made me sick for the whole day every day.

Not that the people at the school weren't nice. They were nice. But after a few weeks I could see they weren't helping her either, and that we weren't helping her by making her go. I wanted to kidnap her, take her away to a place where it didn't matter if she talked except that I didn't know of such a place.

On weekends I took her with me everywhere. The grocery store, the hardware store, the art supply store, the galleries. She'd sit on my shoulders kicking her heels against my chest and hanging onto my hair with her little fists, staring at people. They'd smile and coo at her, talk baby talk to her, though by then she was no baby. They'd offer her cookies. She'd take them and eat right in front of them, dropping crumbs in my hair, without cracking so much as a hint of a smile.

I knew what they thought. I didn't care that everyone thought she was strange. *Still waters run deep,* I'd think to myself, swinging her down and planting a kiss on her silky head as I brushed the crumbs out of my hair. Sometimes I even took her to see Karen. I suppose I shouldn't have done that. I recognize that now. It was wrong, or as I was told one day as a still-hot toaster came flying at my head, *fucking inappropriate.* Mea culpa.

It's just that from early on I felt that May was my witness, you could call it, the one who made my life real just by being there. The fact that she didn't talk didn't matter, in fact it made our relationship deeper. Commenting was not the point. I knew what people had to say about me. Roxanne, April, my parents, especially my father, my sister Joan, Pastor fucking Gary, even Karen. They all thought I was some version of a jerk, and most of them had a lot to say about it. But not May. Roxanne said I exploited her, took advantage of her silence, but that's not true. The opposite is true. I took care of her and if there was something about her silence that made me feel safe, well then OK, she took care of me too.

Roxanne, of course, would say the real reason I felt close to May is that she was the only one who couldn't tell me what a selfish horse's ass I was. In fact that's exactly what Roxanne did say. But that wasn't it or it wasn't all of it. May and I understood each other, and it wasn't even just because we were the losers in the family, the genetic outsiders, the bottom of the pecking order. We had a bond. I'd sit with her while she ate. I'd dress her, comb her hair. Sometimes when I rehearsed, on guitar or keyboard, she'd stand on the chair behind me and put her face against my back and hum. Some people might have thought that was weird, but I understood. I thought it was nice.

I loved to give May baths. Sometimes we took baths together. Sometimes when she was small I'd fill the tub with warm water and squirt dish soap in to make bubbles and just plop her in with me. For one thing it was easier. I didn't have to kneel on the floor next to the tub, hurting my back and getting my shirt sleeves wet and worrying about her slipping out of my hands and knocking her head on the faucet or sliding underwater when I went for a towel. I'd just sit back in the hot water with her between my knees, sometimes with a cold beer in hand, or something stronger, and soak while she'd slap the water with her hands and hum. The sight of her from behind like that, wet and happy, her narrow shoulders shiny with soap, made me weak with contentment.

Sometimes I'd hold her small wedged almost arch-less feet and she'd squat and try to stand up on my hands, waving her arms to get her balance. I loved holding her feet. Of her many adorable baby body parts I think I loved her feet best. They were so solid and thick and short, so brown on top and so pink on the bottom. I could enclose them both in one of my hands.

I know what some of you are thinking. People assume terrible things about a man who tends to his daughter's body this way, especially a daughter who acts as strange as mine did, who is not his own flesh and blood. Did I touch her that way? Never. Did my penis, floating like a pale shell-less turtle in the bathwater, a harmless pink Magellan, brush against her back by mistake as we lay together in the tepid water, like some unknown repulsive sea creature that had slithered up from its nest in the muck to bite the children's toes and spoil their day at the beach? I don't know. I hope not. But even if it did, so what? What would that matter? I never noticed.

But did she notice? you ask. *Did she fear it?* Did she fear me, is what you mean.

No. Why would she? I didn't do anything to her. I never imposed myself on her. I didn't want to, and even if I had wanted to I wouldn't have. Though I saw how easy it would be to cross that line if someone wanted to. She was so trusting. No one had ever trusted me the way she did. I felt her small slick body belonged to me. But all I did was love her.

Don't get me wrong—I loved both my girls, as I thought of them. It's just that April didn't need me the way May did. She had Drake and even without him the whole world loved her. Especially when she got to school. And that was all right, I understood. I even understood when she began to be embarrassed by me. It hurt, but I understood. She wanted to win and we were in her way. She was president of her fourth grade class, president of the Sunday Sunshine Club, first in her Saturday class at the Lycée Français, Clara in the *Nutcracker*. Even at nine or ten I knew she was ashamed of us. I didn't blame her, I was proud of her. But the more she shone the farther behind May fell. I felt I was all May had.

People who noticed how close May and I were—the guys in the band, my parents, the people at my gallery—asked why I didn't have my own kids. They wanted to know why I was raising *other men's children*, but I didn't see it that way. All I could tell them was that I did have kids. *These are my kids, my girls*, I'd say, putting my arms around them both until April started shrugging out from under, rolling her shoulders back like the dancer she was and smiling in that scary tooth-baring way she'd developed and saying that *actually* I was her *stepfather*—God, I hated that word—and that her *real father* lived in Connecticut, Hong Kong and London.

Awkward as those conversations were, I didn't regret not having kids the usual way. I had no particular faith in my genes. At the age when a man should have children I did everything I could to prevent it, and my closest call, when Roxanne miscarried, came when a baby was the last thing I wanted. To invent some new person just for the pleasure of watching it grow made no sense to me, especially when there were already so many children who needed fathers. I had no desire to reproduce my sorry self, would have taken no pleasure in watching some younger version of me grow up. I would have been afraid—what if it turned out like me? But April and May were already here, and they needed someone to cook them breakfast.

Of course as April grew up she found what she needed away from home. Some people are like that, most people are, I suppose, and April was better at it than most. April needed more praise and attention than we could provide and she learned how to get it at school. We were happy for her.

We, I say. Yes, we. Despite all our problems and notwithstanding Karen, Roxanne and I stayed together.

April

D<small>ear</small> Diary,

I love you! You are my favorite birthday present! Mrs. Crowe gave you to me. I love it that you are aubergine with gold letters which is my favorite color combination. I can't wait to tell you everything. I know we will be best friends. I'm going to write to you every night and you will be like a blog except better because I can tell you all the secret things I would never put online. I already have a diary but it doesn't have a zipper and a key like you do. Let me tell you all about me.

My name is April Joy Reynolds and I am eleven years old starting today. I am in fifth grade. Mrs. Crowe is my teacher. I love Mrs. Crowe. Today is my birthday. I have long straight blonde hair but sometimes I wear it in French braids so when I take it out it's curly. I have big blue eyes and high cheekbones. My Grammy Elizabeth says I am going to have a dancer's body like hers used to be. I weigh eighty-one pounds but I'm going to lose five more.

I am an only child. We live in Park View and I visit my father in Connecticut every summer except now he's in Hong Kong and when he comes to Chicago I stay at his hotel. I love it. It's great. You can order room service whenever you want. You can order anything even if it's not on the menu. Once I ordered waffles with cantaloupe and hot fudge and they brought it with a little pitcher of real maple syrup on the side I didn't even ask for and butter in the shape of animals. It was so good but I only ate half because I'm on a diet. I'm going to go live with my dad for a year in London next year or the year after depending. He's going to bring me over. This is a secret nobody knows yet except Dad and me. And now you! Don't tell! I can't wait! I will have a pony when I go there. His name is Derek but he won't live with us. My dad sent pictures of him already and he is really beautiful and cute. I already know how to ride. I have a horse named Charlie at my grandparents' house but he's old. At my house here I have a dog named Mr. Cosmo who is a rare breed called Weimaraner and a turtle named Magellan. I also have two Scottish terriers at my grandparents house named Morris and Boris who are very old. At my father's house in Connecticut I have a cat named Sarah N'Dipity but we may not get to take her to London because of quarantine laws.

À bientôt!

Love, April.

P.S. Every day I'm going to learn a new word and write it down here. Today's word is frittata. It means Italian omelet. Craig made me one for breakfast this morning.

Dear Diary,

Today's word is scoliosis. Sara Wong has it and has to be in a brace.

Here's some more about me, chapter two.

I am in the gifted program at my school. I'm the smartest one in my class. Gerald Partridge is the smartest boy but I'm smarter than he is. They test you for giftedness in fourth grade. My grandparents hired a tutor to make sure I'd get in but I would have anyway. They rate you on what you're gifted in. I was in the ninety-sixth or higher percentile in six out of eight of the intelligences. You weren't supposed to see it but Mom showed it to me. I was highest in interpersonal and linguistic and almost as high in kinesthetic. The only ones under ninety-six were numerical and spatial but I was still in the nineties. My mom says who cares about math it doesn't matter because you can always hire a bean counter. Creativity is what matters.

The best thing about being gifted is they let you do whatever you want. It's worse to be in the regular class because they make you study things even if you're not good in them or it's boring and you don't like it. They make you read kids books instead of adult books like I read. I would hate that. It would be so demeaning. In gifted they let you out of regular class because supposedly you already know it which in my case I do. Although I'm not so sure about Gerald. Then you do projects on your own. I feel sorry for my friend Rebecca who didn't make it into gifted. My Grandma Elizabeth says Rebecca doesn't have what it takes.

The other great thing about gifted is ACI, the arts cluster initiative. You get to do all the arts but every year you pick two and focus on them. I picked performing arts and music this year. I felt a little bad because I know Craig wanted me to pick visual arts but Mom said don't listen to him just do what you want. She says whatever you do don't grow up to be like Craig. As if I'd want to! Nobody ever buys his paintings or even looks at them. Performing arts is much better. I want to be an actor or a lawyer like my Dad or a translator at the United Nations.

Alors, à bientôt,
Love, April.

Dear Diary,

The word for today is meritocracy. It's basically the gifted program but for adults.

It's already the third day and I haven't told you about my teacher yet. I love Mrs. Crowe. I love going in early to help her set up the room and write things on the board. She lets me put up decorations and I water the plants and feed the chameleon Hermes. She let me name him. Sometimes when she's busy she even lets me grade the other kids' papers with her red pen. Gerald isn't as smart as everybody thinks. My favorite thing is every morning she lets me write the quote of the day on the board. I memorize them usually. "The only thing we have to fear is fear itself." President Franklin D. Roosevelt. "Believe in the beauty of your dreams." Eleanor Roosevelt. They were married to each other. "If at first you don't succeed, try, try again." Thomas H. Palmer. From now on I'm going to sign my name April J. Reynolds.

After I write the quote on the board we put out the supplies and then the kids come in and after the pledge of allegiance on Tuesday and Thursday I get to go to the auditorium for voice lessons while everybody else does spelling. I get to skip it because I won the spelling bee.

Mrs. Crowe says I'm a ball of energy and a beam of light. She brings breakfast for us in a mini shopping bag every morning. She usually brings bagels but sometimes she brings sweet rolls. She says we need our protein so she also brings cream cheese or hard-boiled eggs. She keeps little containers of salt and pepper in her desk for the eggs. She also brings fruit either oranges or bananas and we eat at her desk. She puts out special yellow napkins and she brings two thermoses one with coffee for herself and one with tea with milk in it for me. She says I'm too young for coffee, it might stunt my growth. I don't tell her Craig makes me a latte every morning.

I love to eat breakfast with Mrs. Crowe. I never tell her I already ate with Craig. She feels sorry for me because my parents are divorced. She thinks I have to do everything for myself even though I don't. Craig gets up early every day and makes me breakfast and sits with me so I have to eat. Usually he cooks scrambled eggs but sometimes he makes French toast. Then I throw up so I can eat with Mrs. Crowe. And so I won't get fat like my mother or like Phoebe who is really fat. I flush the toilet when I'm throwing up so he won't hear but usually he's washing the dishes so he wouldn't hear anyway. Then Craig drives me to school. There's a bus but I don't take it.

After school I stay for practice and clubs. This year so far I am in soccer, ballet, chorus, French club and violin. I had the lead in the school play. We put on *Beauty and the Beast* and I played Belle. I knew I'd get the lead because I'm the only girl in the school who can act AND sing AND dance AND remember all the words to all the songs AND the lines to the play. Also because I am the best at all of those things. Katie Wolf tried out but she forgot the words to her song.

Craig came to school on parent night with my mother. I didn't want him to because he's not my father but my mother said it was important for him to be involved. When he found out I had the lead in the play he offered to work on the sets. I was embarrassed when he told me but it turned out all right because Mrs. Crowe said he seemed like a nice young man and he built the castle set and it was way better than the kids would have built. He also made the beast's mask out of paper-mache. He and Grandma Jack came to the dress rehearsal in the afternoon and clapped really loud after every song I sang. Mostly the only people at the dress rehearsal were other teachers and the school nurse. That was also kind of embarrassing especially when Craig told Mrs. Crowe it was so good it made him cry.

My mother came to opening night. She got all dressed up and sat with my father who flew in as a surprise from New York wearing a suit. I was so proud of him! He looked so handsome! My grandparents came too and brought flowers and yelled Brava! at the end. Grandma Elizabeth wore her fur coat and afterward she gave me an engraved necklace with a diamond star on it that said OUR SHINING STAR. It's really nice. I felt kind of bad for Craig even though I was glad he wasn't there. He had to stay home to babysit. But he says it's OK because he doesn't own a suit so it's better my mother came with my dad. Afterward we went out to dinner at my grandparents' club. We were going to take the leftovers home to Craig but we forgot and left them on the table.

That's all for tonight dear diary. Good night, sleep tight.

Affectionately yours, April J. Reynolds
P.S. Here's today's quote of the day. The best angle from which to approach any problem is the try-angle. Author Unknown.

ROXANNE

May's pediatrician told us to talk to her all the time, to stimulate speech, so that's what we did. We'd sit her up in her high chair in the kitchen and talk and talk. Sometimes we'd disagree, that's true, argue even, but that's only natural. I thought it was good, she was hearing language at it richest and most expressive.

As she got older and still wasn't speaking we encouraged her to listen as April rehearsed her parts in school plays—she had the lead every year—and recited Bible verses—she won the Sunday school verse memorization contest three years in a row until they disqualified her and made her an honorary judge. We thought it would be good for May, that she'd soak up April's brilliance and have a head start when she did start talking. We kept the radio on in the kitchen all the time—only public radio, of course—and when I was alone with May I made a point of talking to her about everything I was thinking. It never occurred to me it wasn't the right thing to do. I always thought what a rich environment for my little girl to grow up in. I can't wait to hear what she'll have to say when she finally speaks up.

When she still hadn't started to talk by the time she was supposed to begin kindergarten we decided to hold her back for a year. *Don't force her, she'll catch up on her own*, Craig kept saying, and at the beginning I agreed. Only later did I start to think something was wrong.

It wasn't just that she didn't speak. She didn't smile either, at least not often and not at the usual things. Instead of beaming at me and at everyone else around her to get their attention, the way April had, May just stared. She watched us like a little judge, her black eyes following us everywhere. Even when I put her down for a nap on my bed and fell asleep next to her, with pillows propped around us so she wouldn't roll off, when I woke up she'd be wide awake, staring at me again. I have to admit I found it disturbing.

Stranger still, we knew she could smile, she just didn't, at us that is. Instead, she smiled when she was alone. She smiled at her Cheerios—kissed them even—made little whispers and shushing sounds at them, and at the trees outside the window when they moved in the wind. She smiled at April's turtle, which she carried around the house in her pocket even though she knew she wasn't allowed to, and fed it things off her plate when she thought we weren't looking. She smiled at Mr. Cosmo and he smiled back. Sometimes she smiled at nothing at all.

I'd walk into a room and find her standing up in her playpen smiling and humming. Then when she saw me the smile would just disappear. It tore at my heart, really. It pained me, not only that she wouldn't smile at me but that she looked so happy to be alone. I thought what will happen to this child when she has to go to school if the only thing that makes her happy is to be left alone. The sad thing was that she had a beautiful smile too, broad and calm, but when she saw me it was like a window shade had been drawn down over her face. To be honest, it broke my heart. I loved this child, you understand. I was happy to see her. Why wasn't she happy to see me?

People noticed, of course, and thought it was strange. I stopped having anyone over who might say something thoughtless. Except for Elizabeth, who I had to ask in when she came to pick up April. "What will you do with that unfortunate child," she'd said once, watching as May silently gobbled some expensive treat Elizabeth had brought, her little throat pulsing as she worked to swallow it as fast as she could. At moments like these she looked almost feral. "Just love her I guess," I'd said, too tired to think of anything more clever. Elizabeth didn't even pretend to smile at that, just shook her head.

I thought the way to May's secret life was April. She lit up when April was there, watched her every move. I'd send April to her with pudding cups, Maurice Lenell pinwheel cookies, those cheese crackers she liked so much, rather than take them myself because I wanted them to be close. April started to give her food from her own plate—I thought it was sweet that she would share that way—and May would eat it all, her own and April's. I knew she was gaining too much weight but food seemed to be a bond between them so I allowed it. I didn't have the heart to say no to her, she wanted so little.

I sent April to her with little toys, too, dolls and stuffed animals; she liked the animals better than the dolls. She bashed the dolls' faces, cut their hair, magic markered out their eyes. *Nothing so unusual about that*, the psychiatrist I took her to said, but I had to wonder. She seemed unusually uninterested in any human-looking toy.

Even better than stuffed animals she liked real ones. Not only Cosmo and Magellan but any animal, it didn't have to be soft or cuddly or cute. She liked worms. She liked June bugs, ants. She liked the spiders in the bathtub, the mice in the basement. She liked squirrels, loved the neighborhood cats, and all the suburban wildlife. And they liked her. Once when she was about five I found a chipmunk nesting in her room. She'd put out a little supply of crackers for it; small hard chipmunk turds were scattered all around. Who knew how long she'd had him there. For a while Craig went back to drawing grubworms and kept a terrarium-full in his studio and we'd find her in there stirring the sand with her fingers and letting them slink up her arms.

In the meantime April was becoming a star. We were all proud of her. There wasn't anything she didn't do well, she was so bright. She didn't only get the lead in every school play, she was nearly fluent in Chinese, excelled at soccer, French, math even. She played first violin in the school orchestra. She was on the gymnastics team. April wanted to be best at everything and usually she was. April was a natural leader.

Teachers' conferences were always the same. I don't think anyone ever said a single thing about her that wasn't exceptionally positive. There were occasional behavior issues, of course, but always they were the result of April's superior gifts, what the teachers described as her perfectionism, her need to lead others, her extraordinarily high standards. There were funny little misunderstandings, of course. There was the time she told her fourth grade teacher she was an only child. She said she'd had a younger sister who died.

I found this out at a parent-teacher conference. The teacher said *I'm so sorry to hear about your younger daughter* and I said *It's all right, I'm sure she'll start to talk soon* and she looked at me with the saddest expression.

I had to laugh. I realized what must have happened because something like it had happened the year before. I explained that May was just fine and the teacher said *Well I'm glad but that's strange. She swore to me she was an only.* Then she started talking about what a highly imaginative and ambitious child April was. So you see that even when April did something questionable it came from her strengths.

And April was so high-spirited, so competitive. I remember once standing on the sidelines at one of her soccer games as she ran back and forth all red-faced and screaming, pumping her arms up and down and finally kicking the winning goal, and the coach turned to me and said *Mrs. Reynolds, I can't tell you what a pleasure it is to have your daughter on the team. She's one in a million. She's a girl who knows the difference between trying and winning.*

I tried to involve Drake as much as I could in school meetings and activities, and he was usually cooperative, sometimes even planning his trips around school conferences or joining in on speakerphone. I preferred that to bringing Craig. Frankly, Drake made a better impression. And after all, April was his child. When teachers met him they understood better about April, why she was the way she was.

APRIL

Dear Diary,

Happy Twelfth Birthday to me! It's been a whole year since we met and what a year! I've learned at least 365 new words not counting Chinese and French. Today's word is sumptuous, which is the kind of day I'm having. Later Grandma Elizabeth is taking me to a spa.

I'm sorry it's been so long since I've written but it's been quite a busy month. My best birthday present this year is a secret I can tell only you. As soon as school lets out I'm definitely going to London. Finally. Daddy says he's going to call Mom pretty soon and tell her. We're pretending it's a surprise so we don't hurt her feelings and if she gets upset we'll say I'm only going for a few weeks but then I can just stay.

Ciao,

Your dear friend always and close confidante,
AJ Reynolds.

Roxanne

The first thing I remember them asking me when I came to was where she got the gun. I said what are you talking about? Where are my children? And they kept asking about a gun and finally I heard someone say *ma'am we believe one of your children is the shooter. We believe she found the gun in your home.*

There must be some mistake, I said. There are no guns in my house. I don't allow them in the house. I don't believe in guns. Where are my children?

CRAIG

Roxanne wouldn't let me have a gun. She said as long as she paid the bills she made the rules. Though she didn't pay all the bills. By then I had a part-time job as a junior associate butcher trainee in the meat and fish department at Jewel. And I had a gallery representing me. My career hadn't exactly taken off, but they sold the occasional painting and I still had my teaching and playing gigs and when money got really tight I dealt a little. I paid the interest on my credit cards every month. I bought groceries. I bought my own art supplies not to mention other unmentionables. But never mind. Roxanne liked to be in charge. Mostly I went along with it unless I really wanted something. Then I just didn't tell her.

I was cruising the galleries one Saturday morning when I saw Marjorie McCartney's new shotgun paintings. Now there's someone whose career had definitely taken off. I knew her in grad school, nice-looking girl. Her thing was painting on metal and for years she'd been stomping on her paintings in stiletto heels but lately she'd started shooting holes in them. I have to say it intrigued me, in the usual way girls with guns did of course, but in other ways too. My work had gotten too safe, too domestic-looking. I wanted to bust it up.

I thought about it for a few weeks and then one day on the way home from work I took a detour past Wal-Mart and picked up a nice little .22. Revolver. Single barrel. My little secret. Two weeks later I went back and bought another one, bigger this time, a .32. I figured I'd want different-sized holes.

When Roxanne was at work and the girls were at school I'd go to the target range in Waukegan and shoot rounds. It felt good. My plan was to drive up to Wisconsin as soon as

I could figure out a time I wouldn't be missed and go into the deep woods and shoot up a series of metal plates I'd bought on Maxwell Street for almost nothing. I'd already enameled them, smooth and beautiful. It would hurt to mess them up, but that was the idea.

Each one was a buttery panel of a single luscious color, like soft skin tight but not too tight across some girl's belly. Shell pink, salmon pink, butter yellow, yellow ocher, apricot, terra cotta, burnt umber, deep purple, each one the color of a different woman's skin. I planned to shoot the hell out of them. Just to see how they'd crackle. I thought of the project as *Girls I've Known*. I wanted to see the aftermath, the burn around the edges of the holes. I was going to leave them outside for a while to see how they'd age.

I kept the guns in the bottom of my laundry basket, loaded. Why loaded everyone asked afterward. *I'm sorry* I said. *I'm so sorry.* But why, they said. I don't know, I said, but really I was thinking what's the point if they're not? Frankly, I wasn't sure Roxanne wasn't still planning to kill me. I wanted to be ready, and I thought the guns were safe there. It was the one place Roxanne would never look. She hadn't touched my laundry in years. Even the cleaning lady never went near it, Roxanne's orders.

May

April was almost never home. She always had someplace else to go. School, of course, or her father was in town or she was on some vacation with her grandparents or she had some lesson or some club. By the time she was in seventh grade she had after-school activities every single day. I'd wait at the window for her to come home, in the dark in the winter, me and Mr. Cosmo and sometimes Magellan, on the couch looking out the picture window toward the driveway. I'd count the cars and hum along with the sounds as they passed and I'd hum louder in the winter when they made their grinding, slushing sound in the snow. Finally, finally an SUV would pull into our driveway and April would hop out of the back, lugging a huge backpack, and turn and smile and wave to the woman who was driving. She never smiled at me.

I tried to wait to go to the bathroom until she came home. I was afraid if I went I'd miss it when she walked in the door. It was practically my only chance to see her, she went straight to her room until dinner. I made a deal with myself that she'd come home if I counted ten more cars past when I thought I couldn't hold it any more. One time I waited too long and I peed on the couch. After that I stopped—it didn't work anyway. No matter how long I waited she still wasn't there when I got back. Sometimes she didn't come home until dinnertime. Sometimes she didn't come home until after dinner. Sometimes I had to wait until after dark even in the summer.

On weekends it was even worse. She went on sleepovers and church retreats and on those nights, when Roxanne tried to put me to bed, I wouldn't go. I screamed then, practically the only time I made a sound other than humming for the first seven and a half years of my life, and I think it scared her. After I did that a few times she gave up trying to put me to bed and left me alone, staring over the back of the couch at the street until I fell asleep and she could get Craig to carry me to bed. Sometimes people walked by and saw me there. I knew what they were thinking—I could read their minds. *There's that idiot child and her three-legged dog.* Then they'd look away. I could tell the kind ones, they felt sorry for me. The others were just repulsed. *Close the curtains* is what they thought.

During the day, when April was at school or at one of her lessons and Roxanne was at work and Craig was busy in his studio or in the kitchen or off somewhere and Grandma Jack was supposed to be watching me but was snoring on the couch, I'd let myself into April's room and go through her things. I'd touch and smell everything. I'd go through her clothes, her desk, her dressing table with the frilly skirt and the drawers full of sparkly fingernail polish and tubes of smelly lotions. I'd open her closet and touch every piece of clothing, open every shoebox.

At first I took things, made her neat things messy, but when she caught me she threw one of her fits and demanded a lock for her door. There was a family meeting, including Elizabeth, cutting her eyes at Craig and demanding to know why a little girl would want a lock for her bedroom door so I stopped for awhile. The next time she caught me she didn't tell anyone—neither of us wanted another one of those meetings—and just pushed me into a corner of her sweet-smelling closet and dug her fingernails into my arm as hard as she could until my eyes watered—I had a policy never ever to cry—and whispered *If I catch you again I'm going to figure out a way to kill you and no one will even notice you're gone.* She was the one crying, though, not me. *I hate you* she said, *you dumb little dumb stupid imbecile. You are stupid and you are not my sister and I hate you.*

After that I was more careful. I only took small things she wouldn't notice, one bobby pin from the tray, one Milk Dud from the box, one piece of pink stationery from the pad. I ate everything I could and flushed the rest down the toilet. Mostly though I didn't take, I touched. I petted her stuffed animals, I combed her dolls' hair, I opened her bureau drawers and stroked the stacks of perfectly folded socks and underpants Craig had washed and put away for her, which April had taken out and refolded to her own perfectionist taste. I opened the closet and ran my sticky hands up and down the dresses hanging there, up and down the costumes she'd saved from her yearly starring roles. I paged through her scrapbooks. I read her diary.

Then one day I fell asleep on her bed on a pair of freshly washed blue jeans that Craig had left folded there and I drooled a little and when she came home and went to put them on she found a damp spot and screamed and cried and everyone blamed it on Mr. Cosmo.

I should have stopped then but I couldn't. By then I was going to her room every day to read what she'd written in her diary the night before. Don't act so surprised. Just because I didn't talk doesn't mean I couldn't read. The thing that got to me was that she never mentioned me. Not once. No matter what happened, no matter what I did. It was like I didn't exist. Even on my birthday, she didn't even mention me. I had to keep reading, just to see if she would ever acknowledge my presence in her life. If she had, if she'd just said something, even something mean, maybe I could have stopped, maybe none of the rest of it would have happened. For a while I thought maybe she was saving up, saving me for a special story, a long entry she would write one night that began *And now at last it's time to tell the story of my little sister May.* But it never happened.

Then one day she came home and found her diary in a different place than where she'd left it—careless me, I know—and had another fit and told Roxanne someone had been going through her things and said she thought it was Craig. There was another family meeting that night and April cried and Roxanne screamed and accused Craig of things and begged him to tell her the truth and he said he was telling the truth and threatened to leave and she yelled *Please please do* but then he didn't and then they all decided it was the cleaning lady and Roxanne called her up right then and fired her.

April pretended she didn't know it was me, and no one else even suspected. How could they? They didn't know I could read. They didn't know anything about me. They didn't know April laughed at me and said bad things to me in secret and thought it was funny because she thought I didn't understand the big words she used even though I did. They didn't know I'd looked up *putrid odious cretin* in the dictionary or even that I knew how.

They had no idea April was making plans to leave, let alone that I wouldn't let her go without me, that I didn't even care if she was mean, that I just wanted to go with her, get out of there, away from all their fights and the way they were always trying to get me to side with them against each other. They didn't know I was going to make her take me and Mr. Cosmo and Magellan, so we could all be together in London with her pony Derek. I wanted to ride a horse too. I didn't have to have my own. I would just ride Derek when she was busy. They didn't know that if we couldn't take Mr. Cosmo and Magellan and all leave together that I had to keep her from leaving, make her stay, make her mine somehow. Make her part of me.

Do you understand? Her smell was so strong, the light around her was so strong, the humming buzzing vibration all around her made me dizzy sometimes the way the fluorescent lights in the grocery store made me sick and dizzy, the smell of the apricot lip-gloss she wore, the bubble bath she used, the grape gum she chewed, the musical way she talked to her friends on the phone. Her life, her diary was all about leaving us, leaving me, behind. I couldn't let her go. I wanted to keep her, kill her to keep her, consume her, become her. I wanted to be her.

I was much more careful after the second family meeting. I stopped reading her diary. I tried not to wait for her, tried not to be mad at her. They kept asking me afterward why I hated my sister—how could they have thought that? And when she finally came home, smelling of outdoor air and all the places she'd been, the wet snow on her wool coat, the taffy apple she'd eaten at play rehearsal, the cocoa her teacher had bought her, the library books she was carrying, it was all right again and I wasn't mad at her anymore and I'd hum loud, louder, happy as a dog just to have her home and to smell her even though she never even noticed me and went straight upstairs to her room.

APRIL

I didn't know she could read.

CRAIG

I didn't know she kept a diary.

Roxanne

I didn't know he had guns.

PHOEBE

I should have known something terrible would happen that day. It had begun on an ominous note. The first headline was

Man escapes from jail after losing weight

The second sign something was wrong was when Mr. Cosmo showed up in my front yard in the middle of the morning. Keening. I heard him through the open window of my office. I remember exactly what I was doing when I heard the sound. I was editing a chapter on the electoral college for gifted seventh graders and I thought a cat had been hit by a car and I ran to the window and there he was, his face all furrowed, his haunted pale eyes even pinker than usual.

It didn't make sense that he was there. He was old by then, at least thirteen though they never knew exactly how old, and his lopsided body had only gotten more so as his spine curved permanently to accommodate his missing leg. He didn't run away any more because he couldn't run, was no longer agile enough to jump fences and slip through closing doors. By then he just waited until doors were held open for him. He was no longer lured by distant smells because he'd gone nose-deaf. He wasn't even out begging for a second breakfast the way some dogs do— he'd never been that interested in food and by then you had to pat it against his face to get him to eat at all. His voluntary visits had stopped years before, now all his comings and goings were prearranged and ceremonious. He was delivered and collected by car. So it was more than strange to see him there in my yard that morning, even if he hadn't been making that awful sound.

When he quieted down, after I went out to him with a bowl of water, he still seemed disturbed, pacing my front yard with an excited yet skulking demeanor I'd never seen. He shook and cowered when I approached him. I had to pick him up and carry him into the house—he was skin and bones by then, easy to carry. I pushed the newspapers off the couch and set him down there and rubbed his belly and his ears, then went to the kitchen and filled a bowl with milk and brought it to him. I held it in my lap and he drank it lying down. I tried to call Roxanne but no one answered.

I polish up the puppet. I should have gone immediately. I knew something had happened. I knew I had to go over there, but I didn't want to. The sun was too bright and I didn't want to leave the house. This is my confession. I didn't go when I knew I should and if I had things might have turned out differently. I have to live with that. I have to learn to forgive myself, I am told. Instead I sat on the couch with Cosmo in my lap and stroked his bumpy pink belly and watched him shiver in his sleep. Ten minutes passed, twenty. I tried to call Roxanne again. Still no answer. Finally I put Mr. Cosmo on a leash and walked the short distance to Roxanne's house.

Here is how I remember it. I stop in front of the house. I don't want to go in. I don't even want to walk up the short front path. Mr. Cosmo doesn't want to go either. He digs his three paws into the grass when I try to tug him across the lawn and makes his body rigid, looking up reproachfully at me with his weird pale eyes, but he is so light and weak and off-balance by now I can pull him off his feet and drag him. He stumbles and finally he comes but with a defeated gait that makes me feel like a bully. I should just let go of the leash but I don't want to go alone. Bill was dead by then—please don't ask about that—and Mr. Cosmo is all the company I have.

When we get to the bottom step of the staircase that leads to Roxanne's front porch, Mr. Cosmo sits down on the sidewalk and refuses to go any farther. I could drag him but I don't. Stay, I say, as if he'd do anything else, and drop the leash beside him. He looks at me slant-eyed and then sinks to the ground, flops on his side and lies there gazing into the distance with a knowing look of dread. I make my way up the steep stairs and ring the bell. I stand in the shade of the porch and wait, panting. No answer. I ring again. Again no answer.

I glance at the dog lying alone on the sidewalk in the terrible bright morning light. I look up and down the street—you're not supposed to leave dogs out unattended—but there are no cars and Cosmo is weak and harmless and it's a typical suburban weekday morning and not a soul is on the street, not a child, not a mailman, not even a landscaper. Stay, I say again. Cosmo eyes me and then looks away, slumps deeper. Furrows his eyebrows, exhales. We are both panting. I should get him out of the sun, I think, but he won't move. I lumber through the side yard around to the back door, hump my way up onto the deck and ring the backdoor bell. I wait. Ring it again. Knock. Nothing. I try the handle and it gives. I enter.

The back door opens onto the kitchen but the day is bright and the house is dark and at first it's hard to see because my eyes are so used to the summer light. The kitchen is hot and stale-smelling—the air-conditioning is off though usually Roxanne keeps it on high. Even as my eyes begin to adjust to the dark room I see nothing unusual at first except that the kitchen is a mess. The floor is sticky. Dirty dishes cover the countertops, stale cigarette smoke hangs in the air, unopened mail is piled on a table. Something bright catches my eye, a chunk of melting red Popsicle in the stainless steel sink.

The mess seems like more than a week's worth of squalor. I wonder if Roxanne has fired the cleaning lady again or if she quit this time. A bluish light glints from the TV on the kitchen counter. I see a familiar face on the screen and hear the reassuringly low rich chocolate voice, consoling and correcting at once. Oprah. The kitchen is L-shaped with a *breakfast nook,* as it was so jauntily called in the real estate listing that ran later when the house went back on the market, making no mention of what had happened there. The nook is off to the side so I have to make my way past a pile of plates crusted with dried spaghetti sauce

155

stacked on the granite-topped kitchen island and step over a dish of spilled dog food and turn a corner before I see.

What I see: three overturned ladder-back kitchen chairs, four dark irregular mounds on the floor, which, I realize, when my eyes adjust, are bodies. A pool of something dark spreading across the floor. What I hear: breath, passing through something wet. It is taking too long for my eyes to adjust to what I see, longer even than it should because it is taking too long for my mind to adjust to what my eyes begin to see. When you read in the newspaper that a *friend of the family discovered the crime* do you ever wonder what that means? Do you wonder who it was or what she saw, why she was there? To borrow a cup of sugar? To investigate a strange sound? To return a wandering dog? Do you wonder what that must have been like for her? Probably not, I never did, but I am telling you now. It is strange. It doesn't make sense. I did not cry out or utter a word because I did not know what I was seeing. There is an expression for what I felt which I now understand exactly. I did not believe my eyes.

I hear another noise then, other than the wet sound, a soft scuffle slap of small flip-flops on the ceramic tile floor and then there, standing in the dark wearing a yellow seersucker sundress and holding half a dripping red Popsicle is May. Her mouth is stained cherry red. We look at each other. One one thousand, two one thousand. I hear the low mumble of TV. Oprah. She speaks the word *abundance*. She makes it sound delicious, redemptive, like a profiterole rolled in heroin. I begin to hear sirens and then for the first time ever I hear May speak. She says, in her whispery little girl voice, "I called 911."

MAY

The first thing I want to say is that I meant to do it. I meant to shoot my family. In the creative writing textbook they let me check out of the library here it says that Aristotle said a man is his desire—don't act so surprised, they let me read in this place, there's not much else to do unless you really like Ping-Pong—and so it follows that a girl is her desire and that I am my desire, or that at least I was, back when I was allowed to have desire. Now I'm an overmedicated patient in a locked ward in an adolescent psych unit and am not allowed desire. But once I was and it was murder. At least let me own that.

The second thing I want to say is that I knew what I was doing. I may have been a child but it wasn't an accident. I knew what a gun was. I pulled that trigger three times and each time I aimed, or tried to. That the gun was too heavy and the trigger too stiff for my small fingers, there was the accident; my shooting it was not. That my aim was bad because I didn't have depth perception because I never recovered full vision in my infected left eye because the condition was never diagnosed because they never bothered to test me for glasses because they thought I'd never read because they thought I was an idiot, there was another lucky detail I didn't plan for. I'm telling you, though, I tried.

What I'm saying is that I was not the dumb pet goat everyone wants to believe. I was not some innocent retard who thought that by shooting a gun I was playing a video game as they so compassionately argued in court. Except for Scrabble and chess, and the occasional round of strip poker in the linen closet with the orderlies, which doesn't count because it's how I make my money here, I hate games. I think things should be real.

The third thing I want to say is that I wasn't sorry. Not at first and sometimes still not now. It's bad, I know, but sometimes I still feel that feeling come over me like a black wave and I think *I'm glad I did it and I'd do it again* but I've learned not to say so. Not if I ever want to get out of here.

I know it's usual for people to feel remorse after they've done something terrible—I admit, it was terrible—but I can't say that I did. I wasn't sorry that I tried to kill them, only sorry that I failed. Though I see now it was for the best. I understand it's a good thing not to have succeeded in killing your whole family no matter how much you wanted to at the time, but I wouldn't call that remorse, would you? I'm sorry I caused suffering though. That much is true. That's not what I wanted, not prolonged suffering at least. I wanted them to know who I was and how I felt for just a minute and be sorry for what they'd done and then— poof—be gone. Especially my sister. By my standards, I failed completely. Or as we say here—*I screwed up big time.*

But, and here's the fourth and most important thing, I never meant what happened to Grandma Jack to happen. She wasn't even in the room, and I wouldn't have done it if she had been. I would have waited. But she came running in afterward and then she was on the floor with everyone else and they took her away and I never saw her again. Much later, when they started to visit, after they got me to talk a little, I said *is Grandma Jack still mad*—I thought she was mad at me and wouldn't come to see me—and they said no but she couldn't come today. Later someone told me she was dead. *Passed away* is what they said. *But it's not your fault.* She died of heart failure. Failure of the heart. That, though, would be me.

I miss her, her and Mr. Cosmo. I don't want to even think about him. I would never ever have hurt him. I totally screwed it up. I thought Mr. Cosmo and I could go live with Grandma Jack when it was all over and now they're gone and I'm stuck here. What a bad joke and it's my own fault. I understand this is my punishment. The ones I wanted to keep I lost and vice versa. There must be some kind of rule devised by a malicious god—whatever it is you want, you get the opposite. The trick is not to want anything. It's sad, or as Brad, the big fat guy with the red beard who comes into this hellhole to teach us English so we can get our high school equivalencies would say, it's *tragic.*

This place is crawling with characters. Brad. Germaine, the only orderly who's decent at chess. Amy, the psychologist, who has everyone convinced it was all a terrible misunderstanding. *Children don't understand death,* she said in court, *especially a child this young. A gun is a toy they see on TV.* I know all about it. I read the transcript.

I let them believe it so I can eventually get out of here but they couldn't be more wrong. It kills me in a way, to be so misunderstood. I did this to make them understand and now no one ever will. There was confusion about my not talking too. They all thought I was *traumatized* by the shooting—they kept using that word—but anyone who knows me knows that's ridiculous. That's when I began to talk, not when I stopped. Though I haven't done it much since, except with the orderlies and when Phoebe visits. What's the point? People talk about such stupid things. And they never listen to you, not if they think you look like someone not worth listening to. Like with April except the opposite. People looked at her and all they saw was light and beauty and they wanted to hear every precious word. They looked at me and saw a slug. Now her jaw is wired shut and they're begging me to talk.

Mostly Phoebe and I play Scrabble when she visits. She's pretty good but she lacks the killer instinct and I usually win. She used to let me win but now I can tell she's really trying. I never let her win.

They talked a lot during the trial about whether I knew the difference between right and wrong. It was in the transcript and the news stories, which I found online. They kept talking about *the age of reason,* the age at which a person can tell right from wrong. I tired to tell them that doing the right thing was the whole point but they didn't get it and after that I realized it was hopeless to talk.

But did you ever ask yourself what doing the right thing really means? Every Sunday Roxanne took me to Sunday school—even though I was an idiot I guess she worried about my immortal soul—and I listened and we learned the Ten Commandments and the golden rule and the beatitudes. We were taught that the meek would inherit the earth and to honor our mothers and fathers and to turn the other cheek and to do unto others as we would have them do unto us and to judge not lest we be also judged but they didn't tell us what to do if our mothers and our fathers did not honor each other and expected us to honor one and revile the other. We were taught to be kind but we were also taught to tell the truth. We were taught not to kill, but we heard many threats to the contrary, and we ate dead animals and in school, where I listened but never spoke, we were taught to follow our hearts and listen to our guts and you won't like to hear it but if I tell the truth I have to tell you my heart and my gut were telling me to kill them. They just made me so mad.

How do you reconcile all that? Reconcile—what a nice word. In Scrabble it's worth thirteen points, not much for such a good word. *God and sinners reconciled*, it's my favorite line from my favorite Christmas carol. You might think someone like me wouldn't have a favorite Christmas carol, that I wouldn't know such a civilized thing, but you'd be wrong. Anyway it all comes down to the fact that sometimes you just have to do what you have to do and deal with the consequences later. In the trial I was given the benefit of the doubt because I was so young but maybe I shouldn't have been.

It was terrible afterward. It was a mess. The blood. The sounds. People were hurt and I was the one who did it. It was the opposite of those nightmares where you do something awful and you want it not to be true and then you wake up in a sweat and feel grateful it was all a dream. I can never wake up from this. And now I'm locked up here and everyone is standing around saying they forgive me even though I can tell they don't. If I keep quiet enough I can still sometimes know what people are thinking. Most of them say they forgive me. Some don't even bother to lie. I know I have no right to quibble, but isn't it presumptuous to forgive someone before they ask for it? Maybe you should wait until they say they're sorry, maybe the person you're forgiving meant to do it, doesn't think they need to be forgiven. Maybe that's the worst part of all, that they don't realize how much I still want to kill them sometimes.

For a long time I didn't even understand they weren't all dead. I even cried a little once, after much prompting from Amy, my psychologist, thinking they were dead and wishing I could bring them back and tell them things, but then when I imagined them starting to talk, I got mad all over again and wanted to kill them again. That's when they started to break the news to me that they were still alive. Honestly, I had mixed feelings about that. My psychologist, who is a kind person who tends to give me more credit than I deserve, says maybe I just wanted to make them be quiet so I could talk for a change. She says I wanted them to be quiet so I could tell them what I thought. Maybe she's right. Maybe I did it because it was the only way to make them shut up.

But it's more complicated than that, and I don't think she'd understand if I told her. I can't even explain it to you. There are too many conflicting reasons that are true all at the same time, and besides, why doesn't really matter.

Maybe I did it because they thought I was stupid. Maybe I did it because April laughed at me and nobody stopped her. Maybe I did it because I was sick of listening to my parents fight, sick of hearing them recite their endless litanies of each other's faults, each expecting the idiot child to side with them, forcing me to choose, to earn their love by hating the other. Maybe I did it because they assumed they knew things about me they didn't. Or because they didn't take me seriously. Or because they never bothered to know me, never knew what I could do, that I was just as real as they were, more real. Special. Maybe I just wanted to show them that. I don't know. Everyone wants to kill their family sometimes, don't they? Right? It's just that I did it. Or tried to. Either you do a thing or you don't. Why doesn't really count, it's just an excuse.

The thing is, the really bad thing is, the wrong ones died. That's my punishment, that and being locked up in this place until I turn eighteen.

Phoebe brings me books and food. She brings an old flame-colored golden retriever that's all white around the muzzle that was going to be put down for hip dysplasia, and we pet her and talk about the dog. At first I couldn't. I didn't think I should be allowed to touch animals anymore because it's my fault Mr. Cosmo disappeared and later died. I know he did—he came to me in a dream to say goodbye. But she said no, pet away, she wants you to. The dog's name, she said, was Phoenix, and she was for me.

But wait. Before we get all teary-eyed about the dog, I'd like to clear up a couple of other things. First of all, it wasn't an impulse. I thought about it for a long time. I knew Craig had the guns there all along. In the laundry basket. Under his dirty underpants. Pretty funny place to put guns. I knew everybody's secrets in that house. Half the stuff I didn't even know what it was, just that it was secret. There was April's diary where she'd written all about her scheming to get parts in plays and lying about the results of her experiment for the science fair which she ended up winning the blue ribbon for, when she got her picture in the newspaper and they all went out to dinner with the mayor except I had to stay home with Craig. And of course London was her big secret and the pony and the fabulous life she planned to lead as soon as she got away from us. Roxanne had Pastor Gary, I guess that wasn't that big of a secret by then, and the secret checkbook she hid from Craig. Craig had his booze and his drugs and his girlfriends and the smelly little remembrances he kept from each one, which he thought we wouldn't notice. And his guns. Grandma Jack had her pills. Those were the obvious things. But then there were the other secrets. Roxanne's crying. April's food, which she kept hidden in her violin case, and her secret throwing up—for one whole month she kept track of every time she puked with a little hash mark inside her closet. Craig had the notebooks where he kept his accounts—he was dealing by then, even to Grandma Jack. There were other things I won't even tell you. Did they think I wouldn't notice, that I was a complete imbecile? That I was blind? Did they think I was that stupid or did they just forget I was there? And then there was my little secret—that sooner or later I was either leaving with April or killing them all.

PHOEBE

I've grown old. Even my puppet wears her trousers rolled. I don't know when it happened. All of a sudden, I suppose, maybe the exact minute I found May with a gun. Or one minute later, when I heard her speak. Or the day after, when I saw her in the pediatric psych ward and realized she was mine because I loved her. I saw an old photo of me recently, the puppet me that is, sitting there on the porch smiling as usual with a wrapped present and a greeting card propped in my lap and a Hawaiian lei around my neck. I was almost unrecognizable. You wouldn't think a wooden puppet would bloat like that. Doesn't matter though. I cut the cord that day, the day I found May with the gun. I didn't want to but I had to. There was so much that had to be done.

The police arrived almost immediately. She must have called them when she heard me show up. Two squad cars came roaring up, then an ambulance, then three more ambulances. Then a fire truck. Then more squad cars. They blocked the street at either end, when they still thought there was an escaping intruder to catch. There was a SWAT team on the neighbor's garage. Another neighbor told me she'd counted eleven emergency vehicles lined up and down the block, not including helicopters. Who knows—I lost count.

I stayed with May until they made me leave. Not that I didn't mind. I did. I hated every minute of it, the fluorescent lights, the policemen, the paperwork, the endless questions, the casual touching by strangers, the sirens, the smells, the guns. Believe me, at first I thought it would kill me too—I still thought everyone was dead or dying—but I didn't even consider not staying with May and after a while it wasn't so bad compared to that pile of bodies. Everything's relative.

We were on CNN every day for weeks. You can imagine the headlines.

I went with her to the hospital, the police station, the psych ward. Juvenile jail, juvenile court, eventually. I was appointed her temporary guardian and then it just never changed. Roxanne suggested it, after the psychologist said it might be a good idea to appoint someone outside the family, under the circumstances. Imagine that, me being anyone's legal guardian, even temporarily. Duane would have laughed. *Guard this, baby*, he'd have said, making a lewd move. I miss that, his lewdness. Duane liked to call it lewdity.

Lewdity: fourteen Scrabble points, though not with May, who'd used her considerable leisure time to memorize the dictionary.

"Oh loosen up," I'd said, meaning it, though knowing just how she felt.

When she didn't answer I'd added, "Don't I get points for creativity?"

"Nope," she'd said, her eyes still down, hidden behind her black bangs. She was focused on her letters, pretending she didn't know I was trying to make her laugh.

It's funny. I thought I was the humorless one. I'd always taken the hard line on these matters with Duane. I'd assumed it was my nature, that this rigidity was simply who I was and why I was good at my job but now I see it was a part I played opposite Duane, a part that has now been taken up by May. What is it that makes us change? And not only change but become our own opposites? I think of the pile of bodies, the sirens, the gun. Certainly that, but maybe much less.

"I know it's not a word, not yet at least," I'd said, to extend the conversation, keep her talking, see if I could get her to argue or at least to laugh. "I just thought if we could agree on the need for it to be a word maybe it could be. Lewd plus nudity equals

165

lewdity. Get it?" No response. "They rewrite dictionaries all the time," I'd added, trying to slip in something educational.

"Give it up," she'd said, still not looking at me, moving her letters around on the little wooden rack, clicking them into new positions. "You're just wrong."

After the sentencing I accompanied her here to this awful place where she's been living ever since. Where else do you take a seven-year-old who just tried to kill her whole family?

Mr. Cosmo slipped away that day and never came back. I didn't blame him, but that hurt. I started calling shelters and police stations the next day. I put up posters all over town but no one had seen him and he'd slipped his collar and I never got a call. Knowing Mr. Cosmo I think it's possible he found a good home. He was old, but he was resourceful. Or at least I hope he did. The last time I saw him he was slinking through the hedge and down the block as the squad cars pulled up. He hated sirens.

APRIL

To say that it changed my plans would be an understatement. For starters, I missed my flight to London. I was supposed to leave the next day. Instead I spent the next three months in the hospital, unconscious. Even when I came to I was so heavily medicated I hardly knew what was happening. Then when I started to remember, they put me under again, for the first of three reconstructive surgeries, and when I woke up the right side of my face was bandaged and my jaw was wired shut. It was months before I knew that half my jaw was gone. Then when they took the bandages off I spent another two months at the rehab place with a bunch of motorcycle accident victims, relearning how to eat and talk. Everyone said my recovery was a miracle.

When I finally went home—to my grandparents' house—I was *good as new* they all kept saying except for a slight asymmetry in my reconstructed jaw that made my smile droop on the right side like a stroke victim and altered my speech somewhat. I was good as new except for the fact that I couldn't ride anymore because the motion hurt my jaw and I had to eat through a straw for six months and even when I could open my mouth chewing was difficult and vomiting excruciating. I was good as new except for the scars, which make me look like a badly sewntogether marionette, though they say those will fade from red to white.

By that time I'd figured out I wasn't going to be an actress. Not with my crooked face. *Tant pis.* It's OK, though. It didn't even hurt to give it up. It was a child's dream and when I woke up I wasn't a child anymore. I wouldn't want that now even if I were still pretty. If I'd kept that up I wouldn't be where I am now, which is at the University of Chicago, pre-med. I got in on early admissions when I was sixteen, even after missing eight months of school.

I've come to terms with my face, with not being beautiful anymore. I just don't look. Women lose their beauty anyway; it just happened sooner to me. Look at my mother. Look at Phoebe. I've seen pictures of how she used to look. What good is any of that now? The accident was a blessing in disguise. It gave me a head start on my real life. I already know I'm going to be a psychiatrist and you don't need beauty for that. You need brains. I'm going to specialize in the brain chemistry of forgiveness.

At first I didn't want to see May at all, and it was a moot point. She was locked up; I couldn't get out of bed. When I left rehab my grandparents moved me to their house, which they'd outfitted with a hospital bed and staffed with three alternating full-time nurses. Everything was reversed—now my mother had to negotiate visits with Elizabeth. I recall a lot of crying and angry whispering outside my door.

After a year or so, my mother and Gary talked me into going to see May. I prayed about it with my priest—by then I was going to my grandparents' Episcopal church—and he said he'd come with me. We visited a couple of times, but it didn't go well. They told me she wasn't ready yet. *She* isn't ready? I thought. I didn't know if that meant she didn't want to see me or that the psychiatrists didn't want her to see me or that she was so crazy she thought I was a visitation from the dead, but whatever it was, I decided that was enough of that.

I wrote her a letter. I told her I didn't plan to visit anymore but that I was praying for her and for our whole family and that I was trying to forgive, which was only half true. It would have been truer to say I was planning to try to forgive her when I felt better some time in the indeterminate future. But she was only nine years old then and I didn't want to complicate it. I told her I knew she didn't have any idea what she'd done and I said I felt sorry for her, which was true, and I said I hoped one day we could be friends, which wasn't. The priest told me I would feel *lighter and lighter, happier and happier* and that I would be *filled with grace and healing* as soon as I forgave her, but it never happened. I didn't know how. He told me to *act as if and grace would make it so,* but it didn't.

It cost me a lot to write that letter. It felt like lies, and I didn't write anymore.

PHOEBE

*W*oman stuck on toilet for two years

"I should have gotten help for her sooner. I admit that. But after awhile you kind of get used to it."

Later the headline changed to:

Charges filed against boyfriend of woman stuck to toilet

The headline drew me in but it was the quote that got me. It could have been me talking about May, about her refusal to talk or to smile, about her smashing her dolls when she thought we weren't looking, gouging little chunks of skin out of her arms with her own fingernails. Ripping up the strawberry seedlings April was growing in egg cartons for extra credit on the kitchen windowsill and stuffing the little shoots down the garbage disposal. Opening the knife drawer in the buffet and standing there, staring at the steak knives, running her fingers up and down the blades.

I saw all of that and more, things I won't even tell you, and I said nothing, did nothing. I looked the other way. Afterward, I talked to the puppet about it. *Don't beat yourself up*, she said. *What could you do? You're not family.* It begs the question though. What is family?

The boyfriend of the woman whose thighs and buttocks fused to a toilet seat because she didn't get up for two years because she was afraid to leave the bathroom was the one who interested me most. I read about him on the CNN website when I was supposed to be editing a chapter on citizenship for future voters, breaking my headline-only rule. This was back in the days when I'd sit at my computer for hours on end unable to work, eating salt and pepper potato chips and shaking crumbs out of my keyboard. When I came to stories like this I copied key points onto index cards and filed them in my desk in an envelope on which I'd written *stranger than fiction*. A story like this made me feel better and not because I thought it was funny. It made me feel less alone. I felt a kinship with these people, with both of them, the woman on the toilet and the boyfriend who looked the other way and brought her meals on a tray. How about a little sympathy for him, I thought. The boyfriend's name was Kory—*Kory from Kansas* they called him, as if his being from Kansas was the punch line of a joke, the ludicrous detail that explained everything, as if this wouldn't have happened in Chicago or New York. Kory from Kansas told a reporter that they led *an otherwise normal life*—I assumed he meant sex— except that *everything took place in the bathroom.*

Everything took place in the bathroom

Finally she wouldn't pull up her pants, the story said. When she became groggy and unresponsive, Kory called the cops. I understood exactly how it could happen.

MAY

They kept asking me why. Why I did it.

I just stared at them. But if I'd answered I might have said I wanted them to notice me. To see me, the real me of bright desire and subtle thought, not the fat dark mute lump of an opaque-eyed, urine-stinking child, but the real glowing me.

That's not even true. I wanted more than that. I wanted them to admire me, to like me best. I wanted them to love me best. I wanted them to love me only.

I would never tell them any of this.

PHOEBE

I love you. Love you. Love ya. That's what they all say now. All the time. I hear them constantly, on the street on their cell phones or in restaurants, in the post office, even in the library where people used to have to be quiet. Who are they talking to? I wonder.

I remember the last time someone said that to me. It was twelve years ago. Beverly said it. Beverly, Duane's *developmentally delayed* older sister who lives in a group home in Indiana, told me she loved me.

She used to work in a factory that made decorative dog collars but she retired nine years ago. She's seventy-one years old now and I send her a Christmas package every year with candy canes in it and two sweaters and a pair of jogging pants and a 1,000-piece jigsaw puzzle and costume jewelry. One year I changed it for variety's sake and left out the jigsaw puzzle and put in a Mickey Mouse alarm clock instead and someone from the home called me and asked me to please not do that again. They said it made her cry and they had to go out to Wal-Mart and buy a puzzle and write With Love from Phoebe on it. Now I always send her exactly the same things.

The first Christmas after Duane died, back when I still left the house, I had nothing to do, nowhere to go. I don't mean I didn't have invitations. I did. People were very kind. I mean there was nowhere I wanted to go. On Christmas morning I got up early, covered the back seat of my car with blankets and Bill jumped in and I put *The Messiah* in the CD player and we drove south on Route 65 through a snowstorm all the way to a little town outside Terre Haute, to visit Beverly, stopping only for food and to let Bill out to pee.

Duane had felt guilty he didn't go more often—he and I visited her twice the whole time we were married, though he went on his own sometimes without me—and I thought it was something I could do for him, a kind of posthumous Christmas present.

We drove south, Bill and I, through the deserted city. I stayed on the surface roads instead of getting on the expressway, wanting to feel a part of something, hoping a beggar would approach my car so I could give him the twenty-dollar bill I had stuffed inside my glove, although none did. We drove down through the city, neighborhood by neighborhood, through Polish, Ukrainian, Italian, Black, Mexican neighborhoods, through the Loop past filthy snowdrifts and homeless men with plastic wreathes stuck to their shopping carts, then farther south past the hulking smoke-belching profile of Gary, Indiana, and finally out of the city down through an endless series of grimy suburban strip malls and finally, finally out into the sweet open land, down through the clean sparse Indiana farmland where crows flew out of frozen fields into the opaque gray sky and then, later, following close behind a semi's red taillights, through white-out snow blowing horizontally across the highway, over the flat farmland all afternoon until we got to the hilly Wabash River valley, as Handel filled the car with a complex aching joy that even Bill seemed to understand.

Every valley shall be exalted, and every mountain and hill made low, the crooked straight, and the rough places plain.

What should have taken six hours took ten and we listened to the *Messiah* the whole way. We got there after dark, after Beverly's bedtime, and it took me another hour and a half to find a motel that accepted dogs.

The next morning was colder and the snow had stopped. I drove from the motel back to the Good Shepherd Home and all you could see were hills covered with pure new snow washed orange by the early morning light. Good Shepherd Home stood on a hill, a one-hundred-eight-year-old brick building that had been added on to three times, with each new addition featuring the worst architectural innovations of its era. By now even the modern parts were broken down and the once-optimistic church enterprise stood like something out of a medieval legend, a castle in which Lady Beverly, or rather, her mind, was held captive by time.

I sat in the parking lot with the engine running and the heat turned up high, sharing my two Egg McMuffins and three orders of hash browns with Bill, listening to the Mormon Tabernacle Choir until it was time to go in.

Then the eyes of the blind shall be opened, and the ears of the deaf shall be unstopped. Then shall the lame man leap as an hart, and the tongue of the dumb shall sing.

Whatever Christmas visitors they'd had were gone. The place appeared deserted except for an immense woman, wearing a pink down coat and a Santa Claus hat pulled down over her greasy blond hair, having a smoke in the cold on the bench outside the door.

"Hi, hon," she said when I approached. "You on Christmas vaca?" Staff, I realized. A long white stream of smoke and breath issued from her mouth as she spoke. She patted Bill on the head with her big purple mitten and directed me to Beverly's building.

I'd called from my motel room and spoken with Jennifer, the attendant on Beverly's floor, and when I arrived she led me and Bill into the day room, past the blaring TV and the clutch of girlish old women in pajamas gathered around a jigsaw puzzle. Another one sat strapped in a wheelchair eating pancakes from a metal plate that had a rail bolted to it so the food wouldn't fall off. Red and gold garlands encircled the room. A small artificial Christmas tree stood in a corner, the weak gaiety of its colored lights made weaker by the fluorescent overhead glare.

Jennifer called to Beverly, who was bent over the jigsaw puzzle. She stood up and turned around to face me. "Doggie!" she bellowed, hustling over in her manly, bobbing way. For a split second I thought it was Duane. I'd forgotten how much they looked alike, moved alike. She didn't recognize me though.

"Beverly, honey, remember Phoebe? Your sister-in-law?" Jennifer said, encircling Beverly's thick pajama-ed waist with one arm. "Your brother's wife?"

"My brother died!" Beverly looked back and forth between Jennifer and me as if she'd just remembered and hoped we'd tell her it wasn't true. Tears spilled down her face, catching in folds of skin. Jennifer put her arms around her. "I know sweetie, I'm so sorry. But look who came to visit you. For Christmas. Look, she brought her dog!"

"Yesterday was Christmas," Beverly said somberly, logically, wiping her face with one hand and smoothing the fluffy fur on Bill's head with the other. He squinted with pleasure. There was no recrimination in Beverly's voice, just fact. Then, pointing at Bill, she said, "What's her name?"

""Bill," I said. "Bill's a he."

"Hi, Billy Willy, Wilhelmina." She laughed at her own joke. She had a deep voice and an old innocent face with whiskers around her mouth. She was wearing flannel pajamas with pictures of candy canes on them. I couldn't get over how much she was like Duane, even her sense of humor.

"I'm sorry I'm late for Christmas," I said, holding out the wrapped present I'd brought. Beverly accepted it matter-of-factly and began tearing off the paper, uncovering a gift basket I'd assembled from food neighbors had left on my porch.

Beverly beamed. "Look, Jennifer! Cheese!" she said in her deep voice, holding up a cheese ball.

She grabbed me suddenly, enclosing me in a surprisingly muscular hug. "I remember you now. I love you," she said.

Then she pushed me away, holding me at arm's length to study my face. "What's your name again?" She sounded suspicious. She didn't wait for an answer, drew me back to her. "Come here," she said. "I love you." She pronounced love wuf. "I wuf you."

Duane would have liked that. Later he would have laughed, slamming the steering wheel with the heel of his hand. He would have riffed on it all the way home. *I wuf you. What's yo' name?*

He would have said it in bed. *I wuf you.* Or he just would have said *What's yo' name?* at the perfect, funniest moment, lifetimes ago, back when everything was funny.

I'd never gone back, but now I thought maybe when May got out of that place I'd take her to visit Beverly. Halloween maybe. I bet Halloween at the Good Shepherd Home was a blast.

MR. COSMO

I didn't want to leave May but I knew I had to get help and by the time Phoebe and I got back I could feel all the poison coming out of the house and I couldn't go in. Then the sirens started and I had to leave. Later I came back and stayed in the bushes and watched and I saw them take away April and Roxanne and Craig and a bag containing what used to be Jack. I knew it was her—I could smell her. Then May and Phoebe went away in a car and I waited all day and all night for someone to come back and when they didn't I walked into the house and up the stairs and into April's bedroom and picked Magellan up out of his tank with my famously soft mouth and carried him out and set him down in the grass. Fare thee well, I said, and left.

I found my way to the woods near the railroad tracks and stayed there for six days eating the feces of small animals and the carcass of a dead rabbit, drinking from puddles. I was weak and sick and couldn't get up, but then a man found me and took me home. He saw me in the bushes next to the jogging path and came over to me and I tried to growl but I was too weak and he knelt down and stroked my head and gave me water from a plastic bottle, then he took off his jacket and covered me. He called his wife on his cell phone and she came in a car and he picked me up and carried me to the car and held me in his lap and she drove us home. He'd been jogging, just far enough from where he lived that he never saw the signs Phoebe posted.

I stayed with him for the rest of my life. He and his wife were good to me. They named me Diogenes, and they called me Eugene. I lived happily and slept in their bed and ate well and when I died a year later they sprinkled my ashes in their backyard next to those of their cat. Now I'm here. The others are too. It's hard to describe. I don't think I'll try. You'll find out soon enough. Don't worry about me. I'm fine. Though I may worry about you.

PHOEBE

What does the guy on public radio say? *It's been a quiet week in Lake Wobegon.* Isn't that what the mellifluous radio voice says every week at the beginning of another reassuring tale of human failure and folly that ends in gently ratcheted-down expectations, in acceptance and love and the eating of pie or home-grown tomatoes, every week providing a small epiphany punctuated by spilled punch, muddy paw prints or a torn prom dress? Applause always erupts after the first line but that's when I usually turn it off. I can't stand to listen any further. The reassurance sounds false to me, or if not false, then dangerous. That calming voice tempts me to believe in it. I'm afraid it will distract me from the state of alarm I know I should maintain. But I can't get that seductive sentence out of my head, so complete and tempting is the picture it paints. A whole week of quiet.

It had been a quiet week in Park View too. The headlines foretold it.

Vatican miffed about women bishops
Family booted from flight gets refund
Cruise ship left high and dry
Hurricane Bertha shifts direction

Even the bad news wasn't too bad. The cruise ship is *high and dry*, stranded not sunk. The cleverly worded headline makes us imagine the humorous disaster, the good-natured rescue crew handing plump old ladies down ropes and ladders, the picnic meals in lieu of the usual fancy spread, the griping of the fussier passengers. It's a jolly little sitcom disaster. Even the Vatican is only *miffed*.

Warily I scroll down. I can hardly believe it. A famous senator is doing well after surgery. A too-fat ballerina has learned to love her body and taken up the tango. Scrabble goes legit. And, my favorite, *Whales might be medical pioneers*. There's *Pain at the pump*, sure, but apparently no animals were tortured and left to die on the Washington Monument, no eight-year-old girls raped and buried alive.

Some days are good. Things have settled down.

Study: Gay troops don't hurt ability to fight
Billionaire oilman endorses wind power
Beatle celebrates birthday with peace and love

The very lameness of this last item, its very questionability as news, is as much a sign as anything that nothing atrocious has come to the attention of the headline writer in the past hour. A feeling comes over me like the one I used to get sometimes driving home from the hospital at night after visiting Duane, when every stoplight was green, the feeling that it couldn't last, that it was too good to be true, but then it kept going until I began to think that the luck was personal not random, that it was a blessing, a sign that for once I had been singled out for good fortune and that my life was finally going to change for the better.

I still look for Mr. Cosmo. Some nights when Phoenix and I go out for a walk after dark when no one's around I'll call his name, softly so the neighbors won't hear. *Mister Cos–Mo. Mister Cos–Mo.* Phoenix watches me when I do this, her orange eyebrows knitting together empathically in the dark. I think she understands. Once when I was calling Mr. Cosmo's name she sat down right in the street and put her head back and howled like a wolf. It was the first and last time I ever heard her do it, though whether it was in sympathy with me or to send Cosmo a message I'll never know.

I believe if Bill were still alive he would have found him by now. But Bill's long gone so I walk the streets at night calling Cosmo's name and sometimes I end up in the park Craig used to take them to, April, May, Bill and Cosmo, and I'll sit on a swing and think of how they're all gone now, one way or another, and Phoenix will lie down next to me and I'll look up at the sky and sometimes I'll think I see a constellation there in the shape of a three-legged dog.

Because Mr. Cosmo's hearing wasn't much good and because I know smell carries farther than my voice, I usually carry a slab of liverwurst in my pocket on these outings, loosely wrapped in wax paper to protect my coat, or a hunk of cheese or a slice of bologna, along with an extra leash, just in case. When we get home Bill and I or rather Phoenix and I sit down at the kitchen table, me on a battered chair and the dog on the floor at my feet, and I'll spread the liverwurst on crackers and we'll eat the food that was meant for Cosmo. It's a kind of communion in preparation for the feast of reunion for which we patiently wait.

I plan for May to move here when she gets out. I've talked it over with Roxanne. It'll be a few years. I hope by then I will have found Mr. Cosmo, though I understand how unlikely that is. He was thirteen the day he disappeared and that was years ago.

PART THREE

PHOEBE

Esmeralda lives with me now. She's been here for almost a year, ever since she was released. She still doesn't talk much, but unless you knew her story you'd think she was just a quiet girl. I hear her with the dogs sometimes when she thinks she's alone, laughing, talking, completely at ease. You'd think she was talking to her friends and I guess she is. When she wants to say something that can't be said in a few words she'll write it. I don't know where we'd be without email. There are whole days I don't hear her voice.

I'm no longer her legal guardian. She's an adult now, she makes her own decisions, and her decision was to live with me. We talked it over with Carla, her caseworker, before she was released, Roxanne and Gary and I. And Craig, by phone. She's still his daughter, too. I didn't want Roxanne to feel hurt. She was, of course, but I also think she was relieved. She says she wants May, Esmeralda I mean, to keep the option open to move in with her and Gary and the twins some day, but I think she realizes how complicated that might be. So for now Esmeralda stays here, and Roxanne comes to visit us.

May wants us to call her Esmeralda. I'm helping her to have her name legally changed, though I did point out that four syllables are harder to say than one.

"Then call me twelve," she says. I look at her. "My Scrabble value," she says, looking down.

"Doesn't count," I say, giving her a taste of her own medicine. "Proper noun."

"Touché," she says.

I try to remember not to call her May, but as I've explained, I'm old and forgetful and when sometimes I make a mistake she shouldn't take it personally.

I'm having a little dinner party for her nineteenth birthday tonight. We talked about it first, of course, about whether it was a good idea. Or rather, I talked. She stared at my shoes.

"Only if you want," I'd said, when I suggested it, weeks earlier. "And only who you want me to invite. If you don't want to, we'll do something else." She nodded in that way that meant she'd think about it and then two days later I got an email from her saying *OK as long as you let me cook.*

I'm having the party, by the way, not the puppet, although she advises on certain niceties such as centerpieces and color-coordinated napkins. Mostly she's incommunicado these days, just sits in her little rocker in the corner and smiles that phony smile. Esmeralda's big gray and white cat Merlin has scratched her dress to ribbons and likes to nap in her lap, leaving her covered with long silky white hair.

We invited six people. That means there will be eight of us if everyone shows up. Can you imagine? Me, giving a dinner for eight? It's only possible because of Esmeralda, and not only because she's doing the cooking. After dinner we're going to read my play.

Everyone says how good I was to take her in. They use words like *forgiving* and *generous* about me and *fragile* and *troubled* and *dangerous* about her, but they have no idea. She's the one doing me a favor. If it weren't for her I'd still be back in the cave cleaning my filthy fingernails with a sharp stick and combing my hair with bark. My idea of a party used to be a party of one, with an extra large pizza and a couple of bottles of cheap white wine. Not that I don't still drink. I do, just not as much. I need to keep my wits about me, to keep an eye on May. Esmeralda, I mean.

I function passably well in the world now if I make enough lists. Here for instance is the guest list for tonight: Roxanne, Gary, their twins June and Julian, Carla, May's caseworker, and Carla's younger sister Candida. Although they might not all come. Roxanne called this morning to say that Julian has the flu. If he doesn't feel better by tonight Gary will stay home with him and we'll be six instead of eight.

I invited Craig in absentia, just to include him. He moved back to Austin, after everything happened, but we've kept in touch about May. When he visits, faithfully twice a year, he stays with me. He said he'd call tonight to wish Esmeralda happy birthday, after the dinner rush was over. His dinner rush, that is. He opened a little Tex Mex place down there, with the contest money, and he appears to be making a go of it. He won some chili contest. It wasn't a life-changing amount of money, not like the Pillsbury Bake-Off, which he tells me he still enters every year—he's got some idea for chili-filled corn bread custard—but enough, along with a loan from me, to get him started. He lives alone now, in three rooms over the restaurant, which he calls Mabel's Table. Or he says he lives alone. We'll soon see. Esmeralda and I are planning a road trip to visit him, but I told her we're not going until she gets her license so she can do her share of the driving. We'll detour through Terre Haute on the way, to visit Beverly. We went to see her at Christmas and as I expected, they got along famously.

Esmeralda and Craig planned tonight's menu by email—it was her idea to make it vegetarian—and I did the shopping. We're both on a diet now—between us we've lost fifty-eight pounds—but we're taking a break for her birthday. She's making everything from scratch except for the lard-free tamales, which Craig had shipped from some place he claims has the best tamales in Texas. They arrived this morning—they're his birthday present.

Here's the menu. Appetizers: tomatillo salsa, guacamole and chips. Main course: spinach tamales, black bean enchiladas, dirty rice and quesadillas with various sauces Esmeralda's been concocting all week. Dessert: Craig's peppermint ice cream cake, with hot fudge sauce. The crust is Craig's original recipe made from crushed Oreo cookies and some secret ingredient Esmeralda says she's not at liberty to divulge. I did the shopping though and I think it's cream cheese.

If Gary and Julian don't show up, the party will be all women if you include Roxanne's daughter June, who's nine and precocious although not as precocious as April was at that age. It will work well for the reading, since all the characters are girls, though I do like Esmeralda to spend time with Roxanne and Gary. I want her to see that it's possible to be happily married. Or if not happily at least functionally, to see that people sometimes stay married and even seem to enjoy it. Mostly I want her not to feel guilty about Roxanne, if that's what she feels. I want her to see that things turned out all right for her mother. It's hard to tell though what she feels. *Feel* isn't a word I hear her use much.

I think Roxanne is doing all right, all things considered. She's walking fine now. You'd never know from looking at her that she'd even had the accident, as we've all come to call it. Though you might recognize her face from the news, if you could remember back that far, twelve years ago. For a few months she, and all of us really, were all over the news, until they replaced us with some fresh disaster. Though maybe you wouldn't recognize her. She looks much older now. We all do.

She and Gary stayed together. I didn't think they would, but they did. He turned out not to be as bad as everyone thought. I don't know if he was a nice guy all along or if what happened changed him, but I do think getting fired was the best thing that ever happened to him. Even he says so.

He disappeared for a while after that but Roxanne tracked him down. She found out he was working as a lay pastor on some cruise line and as soon as the divorce came through she flew to Miami and met his ship and they got married at sea a few days later, somewhere between Key West and Cozumel. Now they're back here, in Jack's old house. The twins were born a couple of years later. *My medical miracles* she calls them, referring to the fertility drugs she used to conceive them. Now she's selling real estate and Gary has a job writing catalog copy for a sportswear company.

We're going to read my play tonight. I finally got it published. Thirsty Whale, the little press that bought it four years ago, ended up rejecting *Write On Real Girls!*—too long, they said—but published the last chapter, the one-act play, as a sixty-four-page perfect-bound paperback. They printed five hundred copies. It's in the local library and a few are still on the shelf at a feminist bookstore in the city.

The women at the store gave me a book party and we did a reading that night. April and Roxanne and I took turns reading each girl's story. Too bad Esmeralda couldn't have been there, although I guess if she had been April wouldn't have come. I was surprised she did come. She was in med school in New York by then; she flew in for one night and stayed with me.

She's still determined to become a psychiatrist although I think she's having a harder time than she expected. I don't mean academically; she's as brilliant as ever. I mean her other problems. Now she's talking about law school after she finishes med school. She has some idea about combining law and medical ethics with psychiatry. It's all part of this idea she has about studying forgiveness, as a science. I don't understand exactly but whatever it is I don't think she plans to see patients, which is just as well if you ask me. She's grown brittle. She's not what you'd call a people person.

Roxanne and I saw her a year ago. The three of us had lunch together at O'Hare. She's doesn't come to Chicago much, but she had a layover on her way to San Francisco. She said she was going for a consultation with a surgeon who thought he might be able to repair some of the damage to her tongue. We met her at the airport. I hardly recognized her. Her hair is so short now—it's already gray—and she was thinner than ever. Of course she still has problems with her jaw. She didn't eat much.

Drake and his family are back in Connecticut full-time now so when April's not in school she's with them. Elizabeth is there now too. She sold the house in Lake Forest after Senior died and moved to an assisted living place near Drake. I'm happy for April—she's surrounded by family—but Roxanne doesn't see her much. It's a sore point.

I dedicated the book to both of them, *with love and encouragement, to April and May*—she was still May then. I gave her a copy, but this will be the first time she'll hear it read. So that's what tonight is about, though Carla has advised me to keep it low key.

Esmeralda

Phoebe thinks the secret ingredient in Craig's crust is cream cheese, which is ridiculous. It's walnuts. Not that it matters to her. Her sense of taste is shot. That's why she's so fat, which is the opposite reason I am. The funny thing is that even when she tastes it she won't be able to figure out what's in it. Craig says to be patient, that we're educating her palate, but I think she's beyond hope.

Phoebe is teaching me to drive. It's my birthday present, she says. Talk about the blind leading the blind. I know why she's doing it though and it's not about driving to Austin. And it's certainly not because I want to learn. Driving terrifies me—the power, the responsibility for controlling this enormous machine. I'm afraid I'm going to kill someone. Did I really just say that? It's true though. I'd hate to randomly kill someone. I can't imagine being one of those shooters, the kids who put on a ski mask and walk into a McDonald's or a high school assembly and start to fire away. What's the point of that? I never wanted to do that.

I can hardly believe now that I did what I did, that I could have been so stupid, made such a mess. I can hardly remember being that person, though we talked about it endlessly in therapy, or Roxanne did, crying oceans of tears while I sat there like a fat lump refusing to speak. I wanted April to come, but she wouldn't. I wanted to apologize to her. I wanted her to apologize to me.

People keep asking me how I feel. I hate that. It's none of their business. I'd never say it, but the truth is I feel embarrassed. It's embarrassing to be a former monster, to be feared. If I were a dog they would have put me down, shot me on sight, for biting the hand that fed me. Instead, I've been rehabilitated, like one of Phoebe's strays.

Phoebe is teaching me to drive so that I can be *normal.* So that I can go to school and get a job and leave home. Go to college. *Like a normal kid* I can hear her thinking. As if that's so appealing. I keep telling her, by email of course, that I'm not the collegiate type and she keeps saying what do you mean? If not you then who? I don't mean I'm not smart enough, I say. I just mean I don't want to. I can't live in a dorm. What do you expect me to do, start walking around in pleated skirts and knee socks, going to football games? Why can't I just read books?

She and Roxanne are pushing me to apply to schools. "I got my GED, isn't that enough?" I said out loud during one of these conversations, pretending I didn't understand why that wasn't enough. Roxanne actually started to cry when I said that and Phoebe gave me a dirty look and patted her arm and said *She's just kidding.*

We even toured campuses together, Roxanne and Phoebe and I, with Roxanne trotting ahead, wearing lipstick and a fitted pant suit and chatting earnestly with the student guide, flirting even, her trim little figure leaning forward in that earnest way she has while Phoebe and I lumbered behind, as all the pretty shiny-haired girls in tight jeans rushed past. I was wearing my usual gray sweat suit.

We only visited schools within a two-hour radius, so I can stay close to Carla. I liked the University of Illinois at Chicago best. If I went there I could still live with Phoebe and ride the train in every day. I liked it that everyone there was some shade of brown, like me, and that you can see the city skyline from everywhere on campus. I liked that the art department is in an old Jewel grocery store.

"The art department?" Roxanne said suspiciously when I told her that. I'd made the mistake of doing well on those tests and now she wants me to apply to Northwestern and major in journalism. "You're such a brilliant observer," she said in that pleading yearning way she has. "You should be writing. You're a writer. That's your calling."

But I don't want to. I don't want to go to Northwestern and I don't want to be a journalist and I don't want to be anything. Craig says I can come live with him and be his sous chef. That might be OK though I wouldn't go without Merlin and I don't see how I could take her. She hates the car. And I doubt Craig meant it. Really, would you want me around all those knives? Actually I like what I'm doing now, helping Phoebe take care of the dogs. That's what I'm good at. I'm even good at keeping the books. Any moron could do that, but still. Why can't I just stay here? Phoebe's getting too old to do it all, she says so herself, and I can't just leave her. She needs my help. She's turning into an old woman. She's older now than Grandma Jack was when she died.

I miss Jack all the time. I wish she were living here with us, just the three of us and Merlin and the dogs. I wish she were living period. I used to wish I could move in with her, before I knew she was dead. She wouldn't make me go to college. *College schmollege*, she would have said, patting the couch next to her to get me to hop up and sit beside her, like a dog. I wish I could have shown her how good I got at poker. She never saw me play. I wish I could live with her and cook for her the way Craig did. But I can't. I can't because she's dead because I killed her as sure as if I'd pointed the gun at her. I guess that's what they mean by remorse. OK, then. I *feel* remorse, for all that's worth, which isn't much. Nine points actually.

CRAIG

I miss my girls. I call them every Sunday. First I call April, who treats me like an undesirable suitor. Usually she doesn't even pick up the phone. I used to leave what I thought were humorous and interesting messages about what I was cooking that day until she told me in that pained precise way of hers that reminds me so much of Elizabeth that my descriptions of food made her sick to her stomach and would I please stop. Now I just leave messages about the weather. But sometimes she does pick up the phone and we talk about her studies or whatever's going on with her latest plastic surgery. I ask her about boy-friends and she says she doesn't have any. *What about girlfriends* I say and she says *Please.* I hope she's lying. A girl her age should have someone.

She never calls me. I understand. I just want her to know I'm thinking of her. Then I phone May. Or Ez as I call her now.

Phoebe usually answers and then hands the phone to Ez who doesn't say much but I can tell she listens because she laughs at my jokes. I talk about recipes. Sometimes I sing. I make up songs about her. I made up one I call the Wizard of Ez about her cat Merlin wearing a fez that I think is pretty good. Or I read to her, from the newspaper mostly, funny stories about animals, food. I try to keep it light. Anything to get her laughing. She has a surprisingly deep laugh for such a little girl. Not that she's so little any more. But that laugh! I could listen to it all night. After we hang up she'll email me. I have to say, that girl can write.

I'm trying to make up for my past failings.

Of course we all felt responsible. Me most of all. I know it was my fault. Afterward I tried to think of something I could do. I even asked Gary, but everyone told me to just go away. So this is what I can do. Stay away but stay in touch. I stay away from women in general now except as friends. Phoebe laughs when I say that, but it's true. At first I had some idea about getting back with Val but it didn't work out. We're friends now, I mean really, just friends. Her son helps me out on weekends at the food bank.

I didn't expect to get this old—I'm almost fifty—but I thought I'd get shot by some girl's husband, not by my daughter. But here I am so I figure I should do something to make up for everything that went before. There are a lot of hungry people in central Texas.

Aging is so strange. I can't believe how old I look. In some ways I still feel like I'm twenty, but I look in the mirror and there's this fat guy that looks like my father. I'm getting a gut. My hair's gray, what's left of it. The funny thing is, women still give me the look. Maybe I ask for it. That's what Roxanne always said. I'm careful not to flirt, though. I'm careful not to lead them on the way I used to. I admit it, I did. I understand now the problems that caused and now I stop myself. In truth I usually don't even have to stop myself. The urge has passed, for the most part, or abated you might say if you were Ez and had an insanely large vocabulary.

My doctor—a woman doctor by the way who suggested we go for a drink some time—says it's all in my head. She says that I'm fine now, that *it's psychological not physiological* and there's no reason I can't *resume a normal life*. I nod my head. I don't tell her I never had one.

Maybe I'm just not ready yet. Maybe I'm on sex sabbatical and this is my version of a midlife crisis. Maybe I'm the opposite of those guys who hit forty or fifty and blow up their lives to screw around, to make up for lost time. I'm making up for lost time too, lost celibacy, lost sobriety. Finally I'm taking the break I meant to take from all that years ago and you'd be surprised how much I don't miss it, how much I get done now.

Mostly the restaurant takes all my time. That and the food bank. It's all I do now that I can't draw anymore. Or play anything that takes fancy finger work. My left hand was pretty badly damaged. I can still cook though. And play the harmonica. And sing, of course. Tim moved down here a few years ago and put together a new band, Grimly Harris. They play two sets at Mabel's Table every Saturday night and sometimes I sit in for a song or two after I close the kitchen. I'm revisiting Leonard Cohen these days. I'm working up a rendition of *Everybody Knows*, which pretty much sums up my view of things. I'm no Rufus Wainwright but it's not bad. I played it for Ez last week over the phone and got a little laugh out of her on the *everybody wants a box of chocolates and a long stem rose* line.

ROXANNE

People ask me how I can still go to church, after everything that happened. They say how can you still believe in a compassionate God? I don't see it that way. I say how could I not? Prayer is what got me through. If anything the accident made my faith stronger. It's Gary who had the crisis of faith. It almost came between us. He stopped going to church with me. I said we'll change churches. He said no, I'm done with it all.

It was hard for me to accept at first. Here I thought finally I'd married a man of real faith, a minister even, flawed, sure, but good and then he turned away from God. I marry these men and then they turn out not to be who I thought I married. It's my cross, I suppose, one of them. But I believe Gary's different, that he'll return to the church. I believe my faith will bring him back. Once you've known God you can't turn away, really. It's more like a lover's quarrel than a divorce.

I don't know what I'd do sometimes if I couldn't pray. It's gotten me through the hardest times. Not only what happened with May, but now April. She's turned away from her family. From me, from May. She refuses to speak to May. I say to her, when she'll talk to me, which isn't often, you have to find it in your heart to forgive. Not because I say so, I tell her, it's not my rule, but because it's Christ's, and she says *après vous Madame*. I love her with all my heart but sometimes she is such a little bitch. Thank God at least for the twins. I am so lucky to have them, June and Julian, they are the light of my life.

APRIL

I don't get to Chicago much. When I do go I stay in Hyde Park with Virginia, my old professor. She lives alone in a five-bedroom house and says I should feel free to come and go as I please. She gave me my own key. Sometimes I stay there when she's out of town. Usually that's when I go, actually. I always see Norma when I'm in Chicago. Norma Crowe, Mrs. Crowe. My old fifth grade teacher. We became close, or even closer, when I was in the hospital. She came every night for a while and read to me, until my mother told her to stop. I used to think of her as my mentor but now we're real friends. She's probably my best friend.

She wants me to stay with her when I come to town, and I did once, but there were too many people in too small a space. Her husband, her grandchildren. One bathroom. I prefer to just meet somewhere for dinner. The best visits are when she comes to New York. Now that I have the trust money I send her a ticket every year for her birthday. We go to plays, museums. She likes restaurants. Don't tell my mother. She's jealous enough already.

I used to call Phoebe sometimes, too, when I was going to be in town, but she always wanted to include my mother. I'd say can't we just have lunch alone sometimes, just the two of us, and she'd say no she feels too guilty excluding Roxanne. So I don't call her anymore. Not after that disastrous lunch at O'Hare.

Once when I was in Chicago about a year ago I went to visit Jack's grave. Norma picked me up at the train and dropped me off at Rosehill Cemetery, under the big arch. She offered to come in with me but I wanted to go alone so she went shopping and came back an hour later and sat in the parking lot waiting for me. We'd planned to go for lunch afterward at a Vietnamese

196

restaurant on Argyle Street that she'd read about, but when I came out I felt sick. I just wanted to go back to Virginia's house and lie down.

I don't know what I expected but I didn't expect it to affect me so much. I'd picked up a map in the office and walked to the gravesite. It's a good thing I got a map—I had no idea the cemetery was so big. It took me half an hour to find the grave. So many dead people, all those Civil War graves, rows and rows of white crosses and then the obelisks and the stone angels and the mausoleums and finally my mother's family's un-scenic little bargain plot in the back by the chain link fence where you can hear the traffic on Peterson Avenue. There were seven or eight stones for people I mostly hadn't heard of and just enough open space left for my mother. Who knows where they'll put poor old Gary when he goes, though my mother will probably have divorced him by then.

I didn't go to Jack's funeral. They must have held it while I was unconscious. I don't even remember hearing about it, and this was the first time I'd seen her grave. It was a shock, to see her name carved into the red granite stone, a shock to see the dates, to see how short her life had been. And the words. *Beloved Mother and Grandmother. We'll meet in Heaven.* I suppose my mother's the one who came up with that final bit of denial and disregard for Jack's beliefs.

Then there was the other stone. The small one with no dates. *Patricia Jaclyn. Beloved. Too good for this world.* I had no idea they'd buried her. I didn't know people even did that. Honestly, I'd forgotten all about it. Her.

What unsettled me most though were the little bunches of wildflowers lying against both gravestones, limp but not dry.

I've never gone back. I'm afraid of who I might see.

I know Esmeralda can't stay here forever. I'd like her to but a young girl can't live out her life with an old woman, which is what I'm fast becoming. I don't expect her to. When the time comes I plan to let her go or even push her out if that seems necessary. But for now I love having her here and I don't use that word lightly.

I don't mean that it's perfect, that it's some kind of happy ending. It's not. She can be strange, stubborn. She keeps her secrets. She takes days to answer the simplest question and then she does it by email. She goes days without showering. I think sometimes she steals from me. Not money, but strange little things. Duane's Zippo lighter—gone. But I pretend not to notice. She's come so far and helped so much with the business. I knew she'd help but I had no idea how good she'd be with money or with animals. I'm at the point now where I need help. This business is hard physical work. Someone needs to mop the floors, shovel the poop, haul the forty-pound bags of food, separate the dogs when they fight—rare but it happens—walk them, bathe them. I'm slowing down. If it weren't for Esmeralda I'd have to hire a stranger or consider giving it up soon.

I started the business ten years ago. I quit my job finally. I couldn't do it anymore after everything that happened. Once I realized I could leave the house I didn't want to sit home and edit textbooks anymore. Bill had already died. That was bad. Then Cosmo disappeared. I got Phoenix, for Esmeralda really, but I missed having extra dogs around. One dog pines for you if you shut the bathroom door; two have each other. So one day I was doing errands, with Phoenix in the back seat, and trying to figure out what else I could do for a living, when I drove my usual route past Rover's, the high-end kennel, and Phoenix barked and I got this idea. I stopped my car, walked in, asked them how much they charged for a one-week stay, halved the amount, made a sign and posted it on the Petsmart bulletin board. Three weeks later I was boarding a pair of malamutes.

It took some fine-tuning, of course. I had to clear all the junk out of the house. I hire a cleaning service now. And I have to screen the dogs to make sure they get along. And they all want to sleep in my bed so I have to keep my bedroom gated. But I like it. Dogs keep me active. I've even lost weight.

During high season I board as many as eight dogs at a time, four past the legal limit, but who's counting. The neighbors don't complain—they're my customers. We all get along. Even our cat Merlin is fine with it. She was a stray I'd been feeding who'd been hiding in my bushes for a year. Then Esmeralda decided to sit outside all day on the ground in a parka with a can of tuna in her lap and that night she walked into the house carrying her like she was a baby. Later, when we found out she was a girl, we talked about changing her name to Marlene but it didn't stick. Now Merlin sleeps on May's pillow every night. Esmeralda's I mean.

Right now four dogs are boarding with us. They have free run of the house except for the bedrooms. It makes having people over a little tricky but we do it so seldom it hardly matters. I'll walk them before the party tonight to settle them down a little, though the minute the food comes out they'll get excited again. Right now we've got Domino, an overweight Dalmatian, Molly, a docile yellow lab, Perkins, some kind of wiry mixed-breed terrier, and Noah, a flood rescue cattle dog with one blue eye. And Gus, of course, who's mine.

After Phoenix died I wasn't going to get another dog. I didn't think I could stand to lose another one. But then the man who left Gus here never picked him up. Imagine, an old dog like that. I called and emailed and got no response and finally I put Gus in the back seat of my car and drove to the man's house and banged on his door and when no one answered I went to the neighbors and they told me he'd been arrested. He was in jail, they said, serving a three-year sentence for tax evasion. He'd known it was coming, the neighbor said.

It explained a lot. So I kept Gus. He's some kind of mutt, a slinky greyhound mixed with who knows what. He's gray and tentative, with pink curious eyes, and in a certain light when you can't see all his legs he looks a lot like someone else.

I like to think of him as Cosmo's son. It's not impossible. Cosmo had all those gender ambiguities—the supernumerary nipples, the testicles that never dropped. Roxanne once told me the vet at the animal shelter told her he hadn't bothered neutering him because he showed no sign of male hormones. Who knows, maybe on that terrible day, the last day I ever saw him, his gonads were shocked into action and he crept off to explore the last mystery of all. I hope so. I hope before he died, if he did, he sired Gus. Though it doesn't matter. Gus is family now no matter who his father is.

I'll walk him tonight after the party, after everyone leaves. I'll invite Esmeralda to come along but she'll be washing the dishes and wrapping the leftovers and will already have taken the other dogs out and won't want to go again. Besides, she likes to go alone, and frankly, so do I. Gus and I will walk though the quiet suburban streets in the dark—these days I wear a little flashing reflector on my lapel so that I'm visible to speeding drivers—and as we walk we'll look up at the stars and if it's not too cloudy maybe we'll see that three-legged dog in the sky, the constellation I've come to think of as Cosmo. And maybe, if I squint, I'll see the other one, the one that looks like Bill. When it's dark enough and I'm drunk enough I see Phoenix too and sweet Helene and all of them in this dark patch of sky over this small insignificant place where I live and where I probably will die.

Craig has his art, which is said to outlive life though I don't know if that includes the art of cooking. Roxanne has her church and I hope it helps and April has her science. All I have though is this, what I have tonight—Esmeralda and wine and a belief in if not a talent for forgiveness and, when all else fails, as it no doubt will, the dogs. Always there will be dogs.